She heard the key in the lock and was tempted to rush out to Mum and plead with her to throw it away, down the toilet, out of the window or down the rubbish chute.

I hate her, she thought. *Why does she have to do this to us? Why can't she be like everyone else's mum? Then I wouldn't have any of this trouble at school and Jordan wouldn't be such a pain in the bum and we could be a normal family.*

She sat up and even began to climb down the ladder, but she couldn't bring herself to do it.

She lay in bed wishing she could do something, *anything*, to make Mum stop.

Look out for other titles in the *Go For It!* series:

Keeping Mum

Jill Atkins

Evans Brothers Limited

Published by Evans Brothers Limited
2A Portman Mansions
Chiltern Street
London W1U 6NR

First published 2005

British Library Cataloguing in Publication Data
Atkins, Jill
Keeping Mum
1. Children's Stories
I. Title
823.9'14 [J]

0 237 52808 8

Series Editor: Julia Moffatt
Designer: Jane Hawkins

Chapter One

Abbi sat huddled in her seat in the middle of the class.
If she kept her head down and her eyes on her desk,
maybe she wouldn't be noticed. Maths wasn't exactly
her favourite subject, but it wasn't just that. Miss Cook
was collecting in the homework and she hadn't done it.
But it wasn't that either. Miss Cook had it in for her.
That was what it was. She had been picking on her for the
whole year.

'So where's yours, Abigail Arnold?'

Abbi cringed as the harsh voice cut through the fuggy
air of the room. She raised her eyes in time to see the
large, bespectacled woman bearing down on her.
She sunk lower into her chair and felt the blood draining
from her face. She heard a snigger behind her. It was
Charlie. Bold, brash, loud-mouthed Charlie, always
ready to take advantage of someone else's trouble,
especially Abbi's.

Miss Cook had arrived and was standing looming
over Abbi.

'Well?'

Abbi felt all eyes on her as she shook her head.

'I couldn't do it,' she muttered.

'What?' snapped Miss Cook. 'Speak up, girl.'

'I couldn't do it,' Abbi repeated, slightly louder. 'I didn't understand it.'

'That's absolutely no excuse!' exclaimed Miss Cook loudly. 'I don't suppose half the class understood any of it, but they still got the homework done.'

Abbi shrugged and stifled a yawn.

Miss Cook stepped back a fraction and punched her hands into her wide hips.

'Ah!' she said. 'Do I really bore you that much?'

Yes, thought Abbi. *You do. You bore the pants off me.* If only she knew...

She stifled the temptation to voice her thoughts.

'Or is it late nights?' Abbi's eardrums hurt from the volume of the demand. 'Too many discos? Too much clubbing?'

Abbi shook her head.

The rest of the class was silent, all ears.

'Out with the boys, eh?' Miss Cook went on.

Abbi would have loved to make up a few juicy lies. It would have kept the rest of the class amused. But she knew it would make things worse. Miss Cook would never forgive her for it. Anyway, the last thing she needed was to be the centre of attention with her classmates. They might ask too many questions – questions which she was not willing to answer.

So she bit her tongue and sank lower in her seat, seething.

'She was out with me.'

Abbi whipped round at the boy who had told the lie. It was Will.

Everyone was sniggering. What was Will playing at? Anyone would know he wouldn't have been out with dull old Abbi Arnold! Now he would have the whole class in trouble. Abbi waited for the explosion from Miss Cook. But it didn't come.

'Trust you, William Smith,' said Miss Cook, smiling.

Abbi stared in disbelief. She knew that all the girls in the school fancied Will. How could you not fancy him? He was so witty and good looking and clever and sporty. But *Miss Cook?* Was she under his spell, too?

Will was flashing that gorgeous smile. Was he going to get away with this?

'You deserve a detention for interrupting the lesson,' said Miss Cook.

'She wants to get you in the stock cupboard,' whispered Javed, who was next to Will, and a few people who heard it giggled nervously.

'But on this occasion...' Miss Cook was saying.

She stopped mid-sentence. She must have heard the giggling. Everyone held their breath. Suddenly, she turned her attention back to Abbi.

'Come on, girl,' she said. 'What have you got to say for yourself, eh?'

Abbi shrugged her shoulders and shook her head again.

'I—' she began.

'Don't you give me that!' yelled Miss Cook. 'Why I waste my time on you I do not know.'

Nor do I, thought Abbi. She gave up. There was no point in trying to think up any more excuses or tell the real reason the work hadn't been done.

'I'll get it done tonight,' she muttered.

'You're telling me you will!' said Miss Cook. 'And you can have extra for good measure.' She snatched up Abbi's text book, thumbed through it then pushed it under Abbi's nose. 'Page 63, exercise 4,' she said. 'Tomorrow morning. In my pigeon hole outside the staff room. Without fail!'

Abbi nodded and Miss Cook retreated to the front of the class.

'Been out on the tiles?' Charlie sniggered.

Abbi ignored her, but heard Grace giggling. She sensed their eyes boring into the back of her skull. She wondered why Will had dared to speak out like that.

'Where d'you get to?' Charlie whispered. 'I know for a fact you weren't out with Will. There's no way he fancies you.'

'Right!' said Miss Cook, glaring in Abbi's direction. 'Let's make up for time wasted, shall we?'

The lesson seemed endless and Abbi found it hard to concentrate. Her mind kept drifting away and she had great difficulty disguising the yawns that kept surging up and making her eyes water.

How was she going to get the homework done? It was bad enough with one exercise, but now she had two. And there was History due in tomorrow and French. She never had the time or the energy for homework in the evenings by the time she had finished everything else she had to do.

At last, the lesson ended. Abbi avoided looking in Will's direction as she left the room, but she jumped as she felt someone grip her elbow. She turned. It was Ellie. Ellie was almost as bad as Charlie when it came to big mouths and making life uncomfortable.

'Having another night out with Will?' Ellie asked sarcastically.

Abbi wrenched her arm free.

'No!' she hissed as Charlie appeared at her other side. 'I'm going to my nan's.'

It was the first thing that came into her head. Of course she wasn't going to her nan's. When she was little, she had been on the phone to Nan or going round her house nearly every day. If Nan wasn't already at the flat they would go shopping together or go to the park. But she hadn't been round there since she was about eight, when Mum and Nan had had an enormous row. At the time, Abbi hadn't understood what it had been about, except that it was something to do with Tony, her stepfather. She had heard from Nan from time to time, of course, and met up with her occasionally, but it had never been the same. Abbi had missed going to Nan's all these years, but why had she mentioned her now? It must have been panic.

'Liar!' Charlie sniggered. Then she turned away.

Abbi escaped. She hurried to the toilets and shut herself inside a cubicle, away from it all. She needed peace and quiet to recover from that ordeal. But a few moments later, she heard the door open and the sound of familiar voices. It felt like she was being screwed up inside. Had they followed her?

But they seemed to have forgotten all about her. The conversation was on the usual topic.

'Who's got any ideas for Saturday night?' Grace was asking.

'I have,' said Charlie. 'Javed and me are going to that new disco place.'

'That's too far away,' complained Ellie. 'But I'd go if I was with Will.'

'He's not free,' laughed Charlie. 'He's got a date with Miss Cook.'

Abbi couldn't help grinning at the vision of heart-throb Will with that old crone. The others were convulsed in hysterical laughter. She heard them go into the cubicles and listened to them calling to each other through the partitions. Always the same subject – boys.

After a few minutes, Abbi was ready to leave. She thought she would be able to sneak out quickly without having to face them, but then a toilet flushed. Too late. One of them would be coming out of the cubicle. She sat down on the lavatory seat to wait until they had gone.

'Don't you think there's something odd about Abbi?' said Grace as two more toilets were flushed. 'What's she hiding?'

'Don't know,' said Ellie. 'Don't care.'

Abbi held her breath. She wished they would hurry up and go away, but they seemed to be determined to stay there for the entire break. She guessed they were standing by the wash basins, probably preening themselves in front of the mirrors.

There was silence for a moment then Abbi heard shuffling of feet and giggling. Good. They were leaving. But then she heard whispering outside her cubicle door.

'Go on,' Abbi heard Ellie say. 'I dare you. Have a look. Someone's been in there for ages.'

Suddenly, Charlie's upside down face appeared under Abbi's door. Abbi's hands flew up to her mouth as she tried to control the racing of her heart. Charlie's face disappeared. There was more whispering and giggling.

'Go away,' said Abbi. 'Leave me alone.'

At that moment, a loud bell rang. That meant the end of break. Abbi sighed, relieved. One more lesson then it would be time to get out of school.

'See you, Abbi,' Charlie whispered outside the cubicle. Then they were gone.

An hour later, Abbi was hurrying through the school gates. As she ran past the shops, through the park and into the estate, she thought about Charlie and her crowd. Would they always be trying to taunt her from now on?

There was one thing she was certain about. She would never let them into her secret. Never!

Chapter Two

Checking that no one had followed her, Abbi entered the block of flats and ran to the lift. She pressed the button and waited. It seemed a long time coming. She stared at the damp, grimy, graffiti-covered walls and the cans and other rubbish that littered the floor. She pressed the button again. Then she noticed the sign lying in the corner, almost hidden by the litter: 'Lift out of order'.

'Not again!' she muttered and ran to the stairs.

By the time she reached the ninth floor she was gasping for breath. She clung to the rail for a few seconds then pulled her key from her pocket, walked to the door and opened it.

'Hi!' she called. 'Anyone home?'

She always called that, every day, even though she knew exactly who would be home.

'No!' called a voice from the living room.

Abbi followed the sound. She found her little brother sitting on the floor surrounded by a jumble of toys.

'Where've you been?' asked Jordan, frowning up at Abbi. 'Why don't you come and play with me?'

'I will in a minute,' said Abbi. 'Where's Mum?'

A look of rage passed over Jordan's face as he pointed towards the door.

'Her bedroom,' he said.

Abbi frowned. That usually meant one thing. She would have to go and investigate.

'Have you been to school today?' she asked.

'Yes,' said Jordan. 'But I hate it.'

Abbi pretended she hadn't heard Jordan's complaint.

'And did Mum pick you up?'

'Yes,' repeated Jordan. 'She was late again.'

Abbi smiled at him. She had to try to keep him calm.

'Never mind,' she said.

But Jordan leapt to his feet.

'But I don't like it!' he shouted.

Abbi didn't argue. She didn't need another flare up with Jordan. She didn't think she could handle it. The last one had been terrible. Jordan had become so angry she had been terrified. It was best to try to change the subject.

'So what do you want me to play?' she asked.

While she played Jordan's favourite game, Rescue Rangers, with him, she thought about how he was so aggressive sometimes. It must be because of Mum. Or maybe Tony had something to do with it.

After a while, Jordan seemed to have forgotten his anger and was playing quite happily. She thought it was time to check on Mum.

'Hey, Ranger!' she said to Jordan. 'I see someone needs rescuing. You go and help him. I won't be long.'

She crept from the room and along the corridor to their mum's bedroom. The door stood ajar so Abbi peered through the crack. There lay Mum, on top of the covers, fast asleep, snoring. Abbi tiptoed into the room, though she knew she had no need to be quiet. When Mum was asleep like this, twenty cannons firing in her ear wouldn't wake her.

Abbi found a blanket at the bottom of the bed and draped it over Mum. She stood over her and looked down at her face. She wasn't bad for a thirty-five-year old. She would be quite attractive if only she would take the trouble. But her long dark hair lay lank and greasy on her pillow and the little make-up she wore was old and smudged.

Abbi sighed and walked away, then hurried back to Jordan.

'Did you rescue him?' she asked in a cheerful voice.

'Yeah! He's OK now.'

'Great!'

For the time being, Jordan was relaxed. Abbi sat amongst the chaos of toys for quite a while and took orders from her little brother. She had to keep him happy.

Later, she switched on the TV.

'Watch that while I get your tea,' she said as she went to the kitchen.

First, she threw out the rubbish. She was glad there was a chute outside on the landing. She didn't fancy carrying that lot down nine flights of stairs. The bag was heavy, full of glass bottles. She listened to the bottles clanking as they cascaded down to the bottom of the chute then she returned to the flat.

Back in the kitchen, Abbi tidied away the breakfast things and cleared a space. She opened a tin of baked beans and made some toast. A few minutes later, she and Jordan were sitting side by side on the settee, watching *The Simpsons*, eating.

There was a noise from the bedroom. Perhaps Mum was waking up. Abbi waited nervously. What sort of mood would she be in? She watched the living room door, but no one came in. False alarm.

Soon, it was Jordan's bedtime. Luckily, he was feeling co-operative for once and gave Abbi no trouble. He let her help him undress then she read him a story and made sure he cleaned his teeth and washed his hands and face. She tucked him into the bottom bunk.

'Night,' she whispered. 'Mind the bugs don't bite.'

Jordan smiled sleepily.

'Will you leave the light on?'

'All right,' said Abbi.

She knew her brother was afraid of the dark. Sometimes he had bad dreams and woke up terrified. She would turn out the light when he was asleep.

Abbi returned to the living room and picked up her school bag. She looked at the clock. It was already gone seven-thirty. She sighed, sat down at the table and pulled out her Maths textbook. She had lied to Miss Cook. She *did* understand the Maths. You didn't have to be Einstein to be able to do it. It was what was happening at home that was the trouble.

Abbi had just found the page of yesterday's homework when the door opened and Mum appeared in the doorway, squinting against the bright light. Her hair stuck out at all angles and her face was flushed and blotchy. Abbi closed the book. She guessed the homework would have to wait.

'Hello,' said Mum, walking slowly into the room. 'How long have I been asleep?'

'About four hours, I think,' said Abbi.

'Oh.' Mum sat down heavily on the settee and put her head in her hands.

'I feel awful.'

She looked awful, too, but at least she wasn't in one of her aggressive moods. That was something. Abbi waited. She had learned that was the best way to deal with this.

Suddenly, Mum lifted her head and stared around the room.

'Where's Jordan?' she demanded.

'It's all right,' said Abbi. 'He's in bed, sound asleep by now.'

Mum relaxed a little then frowned.

'I fetched him from school,' she said. 'Was I on time?'

'Only a bit late.'

'But I can't remember much else.'

'I came home at the usual time,' said Abbi. 'Don't worry. You were asleep and Jordan was playing with his Rescue Rangers. We had a good time and—'

'Thanks, Ab.' Mum reached out her hand towards Abbi and began to cry. 'You're so good. I don't know what I'd do without you.'

Abbi got up from the table and gave her a hug.

'D'you fancy a cuppa?' she asked gently.

They sat for an hour over the cup of tea. Abbi's mum needed to talk. Abbi, who was becoming used to evenings like this lately, was prepared to listen.

'I'm sorry,' Mum began, as usual. 'I don't know what happens. I just can't stop myself.'

'It's OK, Mum.' Abbi put her hand on her arm.

'I'm such a rotten mother. I've got two lovely children that I should be looking after.' Tears streamed down her cheeks. 'And instead, they have to look after me.'

Abbi handed her the box of tissues, but said nothing. She had heard her mum talk like this before so she could guess what was coming next. The promises. Always the promises.

Mum blew her nose.

'I will change,' she cried. 'I'll get myself straight. I'll get myself a little job. Now Jordan's at school I can do that. Yes, a little job, in an office, like I used to – before I met Tony.'

Abbi frowned, but still stayed silent. She hated her stepdad. This was all his fault. Nan had been right. He was a loser, a boozer, a dropout, a stinking liar. Mum had begun drinking when Tony had arrived on the scene. It hadn't been too bad at first, but Abbi remembered the first night he had stayed. She had been frightened. Mum had got drunk. Everything had gone downhill from then on. Abbi had watched Mum struggle since, but she knew deep down that Mum had been hooked for ages.

Then Tony had left and things had improved, but he kept coming back. Every time he turned up he got Mum into drinking again. Then each time he disappeared, Mum wasn't able to cope and things got out of hand. This time had been the worst ever.

'But there's one thing I'm dead certain of,' said Mum. 'From now on, I'll never touch another drop of alcohol.'

'Mum,' Abbi said gently. 'How many times have you promised me that?'

'But I mean it. I really want to kick the habit. Just give me a chance.'

Abbi sighed.

'Of course I'll give you another chance, Mum,' she said, giving her another hug.

I wish, she thought.

Chapter Three

Abbi stared at the jumbled figures on the page. Her eyes didn't want to focus any more. She was too tired and she couldn't concentrate. The TV was on. It was one of her mum's favourite programmes; a quiz show.

'All right and now for the next question...' the question master was saying.

Abbi's eyes were drawn to the screen and for the next few minutes she let it take her over. Some of the questions were so ridiculously easy the neighbour's cat could have answered them.

Maths! She dragged her eyes from the TV and bent over the table again, but it was no good. She would never get it done. The voices on the box kept breaking into her mind.

Abbi felt torn. Mum was going to have a terrible hangover in the morning and would need looking after.

So I could skip school tomorrow, she thought.

It was very tempting, but it wouldn't solve anything. She would only get further and further behind.

She made up her mind.

'I'm going to my room,' she said, standing up. 'I have to get this done.'

'OK.' Her mum's eyes didn't leave the screen as Abbi gathered up her books and headed for her bedroom.

My bedroom; she would love it to be hers alone. Actually, it was *our bedroom* – the one she shared with Jordan. It was ridiculous, a fourteen-year-old girl sharing with a five-year-old boy, not that she didn't love him dearly.

After Dad had died when she was five, she and Mum had moved into this flat, and the room had been hers. But then Tony had come along and Jordan had been born so she had had to share ever since.

If only she could have her own space. If only things could be different...

She sighed and pushed open the bedroom door. The light was still on. She had forgotten to turn it off. Jordan was breathing steadily with a slight smile on his face. He looked relaxed and peaceful. It was good that, in spite of his problems when he was awake, at least he slept well. He wasn't old enough to worry like Abbi did and she wanted to keep it that way.

She sat down at the little table in the corner and began again – two lots of Maths and French. But she was so tired.

Suddenly, she sat bolt upright. How long had she been asleep with her head on the table? She looked at her watch. Two am. Hours! The Maths book lay open at the same page. It still had to be done. She could hear the TV. Mum was still up. Perhaps she was asleep on the settee. She might even be drinking. Abbi resisted the temptation to investigate. She had to work.

When the alarm rang the following morning, Abbi's eyes refused to open. She couldn't remember getting undressed or climbing the ladder on to the top bunk although she must have done somehow. But she did recall one important fact. She had finished all the homework, even the French, about three-thirty am.

Below her, Abbi heard Jordan stirring, so she forced her eyes open and clambered rather stiffly down the ladder and hurried to the bathroom. She moved like a robot, through the daily routine: washing and dressing and packing her bags; getting Jordan up and washed and dressed; then dishing out his breakfast and making their packed lunch. Abbi searched the cupboards. Jam sandwiches would have to do. There was no sign of Mum. She must have gone to bed at some unearthly hour last night.

At eight o'clock, Abbi made a cup of tea and took it along the corridor, but Mum was sound asleep. She left the tea by the bed and hurried back to Jordan. It looked like she would have to take him to school today.

If only she could ring Nan, like in the old days.

But that would be disloyal to Mum, wouldn't it? And what would Nan do? Maybe she would blow the whistle on Mum. Then they might be split up. That would be the end of the world!

No, the most important thing in Abbi's life at the moment was to keep the family together – Mum and Jordan and her – so she had to make sure no one else knew. If Mum's problem got out, the consequences could be unthinkable. So she couldn't ring Nan now. Perhaps, if things got worse...

At ten past nine, Abbi ran into school, having dropped Jordan off at his infant school first. She hurried to the staff room and stuffed the Maths homework into Miss Cook's pigeon hole.

Footsteps behind her made her jump. She whipped round. Miss Cook was bearing down on her.

'So you've saved your skin this time,' said Miss Cook. 'But there will be trouble if it hasn't been done properly.'

'Yes, Miss Cook,' said Abbi politely, as she made her escape.

Mr Lam looked up as she entered the classroom. She went over to his table.

'Sorry,' she said.

'Well?' he asked quietly.

Abbi could feel her whole body shaking. Her eyes smarted with tears. Which lie would she tell this morning?

'My mum's not well, so I had to take my little brother to school,' she muttered, biting her top lip. Well, it was almost the truth. Anyone's mum can get sick from time to time.

Mr Lam nodded.

'I see,' he said. Abbi felt as though he was staring right into her brain. Could he detect that she was telling him only half the story?

There was dead silence in the room. Abbi suddenly realised everyone had been listening. She could hear her own breathing and her heart pounding away in her chest. Could the rest of the class hear that, too?

'Come and see me at break,' said Mr Lam.

Abbi thought she could sense concern in Mr Lam's voice. She nodded and went to her seat.

'You're in for it now,' said Charlie a few minutes later as they made their way to the science lab for the first period.

Abbi moved away. She managed to keep two people between her and Charlie's gang all the way to the lab.

But in science, she was aware of someone watching her. She felt her eyes drawn to her left. It was Will. She caught his eye for a split second. She wouldn't have believed it, but he actually seemed embarrassed.

This is ridiculous, thought Abbi. *What does he think he's playing at?*

But it happened again. This time, he showed just a flicker of a smile in his eyes. She wasn't sure quite how to take it. Small, quiet, ordinary girls were definitely not his type. He normally went for tall attractive types. He must be taking the mickey.

The double science lesson flashed by and break came round too quickly. Suddenly, the bell was ringing and butterflies began dancing in her stomach. What was Mr Lam going to say?

She snatched up her bag and hurried for the door. She didn't want to give Charlie and her gang the chance to make things worse. But someone caught up with her at the end of the corridor.

'Good luck,' Will murmured under his breath as he breezed past.

Abbi stared at his back. Surely this hunk of a bloke, who was like a god around the school to all the girls, couldn't seriously be wishing her luck? He must have said that with his tongue in his cheek, or done it for a bet.

But as she approached the form room, Abbi forgot Will and switched her mind to Mr Lam. She dreaded what he was going to say. She felt her hands shaking as she reached for the handle and pushed open the door. He was waiting for her. He had placed two chairs in the corner of the room, near the window. As Abbi sat down opposite him, she could see hordes of teenagers standing around outside in the drizzle and for once wished she could be out there with them.

'Right,' began Mr Lam quietly. His face was expressionless. He was giving nothing away. 'I think you know why I've asked to see you.'

Abbi wasn't sure. It could be a number of things.

'If it's the Maths homework,' she said. 'I've done…'

'No, it's not the Maths homework,' said Mr Lam, 'although I suppose that could be a small part of it.'

So it's everything, thought Abbi, immediately on the defensive. *What does he know?*

She waited for him to continue. She would have to play this very cannily.

'Is everything all right at home?' asked Mr Lam.

'Yes!' Abbi knew she had said it too quickly. She cursed herself. He would be suspicious now.

'Are you sure? I'll tell you why I ask. Several of my colleagues have expressed their concern about you. You seem to be having difficulty keeping up with the work. I've noticed a change in you. You've gone into yourself. I'd like to find out why.'

Abbi forced a smile to her lips, but she knew her eyes were not smiling. He would notice that, too.

'Everything's fine,' she said.

'And you seem to be apart from the rest of the class,' said Mr Lam. 'You're not being bullied, are you?'

Abbi shook her head. She tried smiling again, hoping she would convince him.

'Abbi, I want you to trust me,' Mr Lam said kindly.

Alarm bells rang in Abbi's head. She hated that phrase. How did she know if she could trust him, trust anybody? She had confided in a teacher once before, several years ago, and she had been let down. He had contacted social services and someone had been round to the flat. Mum had been very upset. She said she didn't want anyone interfering.

'I'm aware that there are a few people in this class who—'

'Everything's fine,' Abbi repeated. If she split on Charlie and the others he would want to talk to them and that would make things worse.

'OK,' said Mr Lam. 'Only I just want to say this. If there is anything wrong, you should get help – not necessarily me – someone you know better, perhaps.'

'But—'

'My advice is this – don't let it go on too long. Do something about it before it gets out of hand. A problem shared and all that.'

Abbi forced another smile then bit her lip hard to stop the tears.

I wish I could, she thought. *I wish I could...*

Chapter Four

When Abbi let herself into the flat that afternoon, she found her mum sitting on the settee. Jordan was upside down in an armchair, watching children's TV. Abbi smiled at Mum and went to the bedroom. She lay on her bunk for a few minutes, taking in deep breaths, trying to relax, to ease out the tensions of the day.

She felt her body growing heavier and her breathing becoming slower. Her eyes closed. She snuggled into her duvet. It was warm and comforting…

She woke to the smell of cooking. She glanced at her clock. It was five-thirty already and her stomach told her she was ready for whatever was offered her. But she didn't hurry down from the bunk. She felt too dozy. It would be great to just go back to sleep, for hours and hours and hours.

'Abbi, are you there?'

Jordan had come into the room. No more sleep for the moment. She rolled over and looked down at him.

'Hi,' she said, yawning. 'Had a good day?'

'Nah. I had a fight with Josh and I had to go and sit in the hall,' said Jordan. 'Then my teacher told me off.'

'What did you do?'

'I wanted to play in the sand, but she wouldn't let me so I chucked a load of sand and some went in Kelly's eye and—'

'Oh dear,' said Abbi. She sympathised with him. It seemed to run in the family, getting into trouble. But she worried about how he was behaving. Soon, they would be sending for Mum and everything would get out of hand.

Jordan climbed the ladder and stood only a few centimetres from her. Abbi reached across and gave him a hug.

'Get off,' he complained, but he grinned at her.

Abbi let go.

'Come up here,' she said, patting the bed beside her. 'I want to tell you a secret.'

Jordan's face lit up. He scrambled up and sat by her feet. She was silent for a while, wondering how she could explain everything to a five year old. But Jordan was fidgeting. He liked secrets, but was he going to like this one?

'Come on, then,' he said, breaking into her thoughts. He still had an eager expression on his face. 'I want to know the secret.'

Abbi wondered if she was being wise, but she had to take the gamble.

'It's about Mum,' she whispered. 'She isn't very well and we both need to be ever so good for her sake.'

He looked disappointed. It wasn't much of a secret to a little boy.

'Why?'

'Because.' What could she tell him? 'If our teachers ask to see Mum—'

'—they'll find out she gets drunk.' He spoke in such a matter-of-fact voice. His face was serious and he was nodding.

Abbi gasped. She was amazed. He was only five. How did he know about all that? He must have heard someone else say it. Suddenly, Jordan seemed much older than five, more like a sage old man.

'Exactly,' she managed to say. 'And do you know what that might mean?'

Jordan shook his head. His eyes were wide and innocent again, back to being a little boy. Abbi didn't want to frighten him, but she had to warn him.

'If they find out, that ... well, you know—'

'Yeah?'

'—they could say she isn't well enough to look after us – they could even make us go and live somewhere else.'

Abbi held her breath for a second, waiting for Jordan's response. His eyes brimmed with tears.

'But sometimes—' he said with a sniff '—sometimes I can't help it.'

'But you will try and be good?'

Jordan nodded.

'And it will be our little secret – just between you and me?'

'OK,' he whispered. Then he leaned closer to Abbi. 'Mum came on time today.'

Perhaps he was thinking of their secret as part of a game. Good. That way, it might not get to him too much.

As he leapt down from the bunk and ran out of the room, Abbi guessed they were all living on borrowed time. Mum was sober today, but how long before she went back on the bottle this time? Then how long would it be before Jordan's teacher or Mr Lam started guessing the truth? She dreaded to think, but she suspected it might not be very long at all.

Abbi climbed down from the bunk and followed Jordan more slowly. As she reached the doorway, she heard him call, 'Grub up! It's egg and chips! My favourite!'

A few moments later, they were sitting round the table, tucking in. Egg and chips wasn't exactly Abbi's favourite, but she was so pleased that Mum had been well enough to cook tea that she enjoyed it. As she ate, she kept stealing glances at her mum. It was amazing, the difference that keeping off the drink for one day made. She had really made an effort. Her hair looked brushed and silky and she had applied some fresh make-up.

Maybe this time she will keep her promise, thought Abbi, crossing her fingers and everything else she could think of. But she knew the score. She couldn't really believe it could happen. It wasn't as easy as all that.

As soon as they had finished eating, Abbi hurried to the bedroom. She would let Mum play with Jordan for once and watch the TV and do all the other things *she* had to do on those evenings when Mum was out of action.

She struggled through her homework, determined not to be disturbed by anything. When it was Jordan's bedtime, she transferred to the kitchen table and worked on. She had to make the most of this chance to keep up, to blow away any suspicion anyone had about her home life. By the time she had finished it was past nine o'clock.

It even occurred to her, as she closed her books and packed her bag for the morning, that she had time to nip out to one of those places Charlie and her gang were always on about. That would surprise them! But there was no way she was going to do that. She didn't have the latest disco gear and the only make-up and nail varnish she had were Mum's throw-outs.

'You never go out, do you?' Mum said as if she had read Abbi's mind. 'When I was your age…'

'It's OK, Mum,' Abbi said quickly.

'Haven't you got a boyfriend?'

Abbi shook her head, but was annoyed to feel a tremendous heat rising to her face as a picture of Will flashed before her eyes.

Will? Boyfriend? Be realistic, Abbi Arnold! Just because he was watching me in science! What was his game, anyway?

But her mum had seen the blush.

'So, you dark horse, you!' she said. 'What's his name?'

'There is no name,' said Abbi, getting up to make a cup of tea. 'No boyfriend. Just the crowd at school, that's all.'

They talked about music and TV and Jordan and things they did when Abbi was little and lots of other things they hadn't talked about for years. Thankfully, there were no more questions about boys or friends, and school was not mentioned. In return, Abbi kept off the subjects she desperately wanted to talk about, like Nan and Mum's problem and how the money they got from the Post Office each week was never enough.

But throughout the evening, Abbi could not help noticing several things about her mum. She was smoking more than normal and biting her fingernails. Then, as the evening progressed, she became more restless. She couldn't seem to sit still and kept sighing and looking at her watch. Abbi knew the signs. Pigs were more likely to fly than her mum give up alcohol long term.

A little later, when Abbi was in bed, she was not at all surprised to hear the front door click. She crept out of bed and searched the rest of the flat. No Mum. She had gone out. Abbi lay awake, racking her brains, trying to think of some way to stop her, but what was the use? There was no way. Life would spiral down and down to goodness knows what.

She heard the key in the lock and was tempted to rush out to Mum and plead with her to throw it away, down the toilet, out of the window or down the rubbish chute.

I hate her, she thought. *Why does she have to do this to us? Why can't she be like everyone else's mum? Then I wouldn't have any of this trouble at school and Jordan wouldn't be such a pain in the bum and we could be a normal family.*

She sat up and even began to climb down the ladder, but she couldn't bring herself to do it.

She lay in bed wishing she could do something, *anything*, to make Mum stop.

Chapter Five

Abbi had great difficulty in opening her eyes again when the alarm rang next morning, but she struggled out of bed. She knew from past experience that she would be the one who had to get Jordan to school, so the sooner she began the routine the better.

The first sound she heard as she left her room was Mum being sick. Great.

'Come on, Jordan,' she called, trying to sound cheerful. 'Time to get up.'

'No!' Jordan's muffled voice came from under his duvet.

Abbi gritted her teeth. It was going to be one of those mornings. She dressed, snatched a piece of bread for breakfast and got the school bags ready. Mum wandered into the kitchen. She was crying and looked like death.

'Oh Abbi!'

She needs me, Abbi thought. *Should I stay at home? No, I've got to keep things going as normal as possible.*

She hugged Mum, sat her down in the sitting room and hurried back to the bedroom, putting on her brightest smile as she gently pulled the duvet away.

'Hey, Ranger,' she said. 'Who needs rescuing today?'

But Jordan was not in the mood for games and it took a struggle to dress him and force a mouthful of toast down him before dragging him out of the flat. Mum had gone back to bed so Abbi felt a little better about leaving her.

'I don't want to go to school,' Jordan complained as they set off.

'Yes you do.'

She felt exhausted, limp as a stale lettuce leaf, after she had pushed him through his classroom door and hurried away. She wished she hadn't bothered. Life would have been much more straightforward if they had both skipped school. It was a fine day. The park would have been much better than facing Mr Lam. And worse than that, it was Maths first period.

She dashed into school and burst into the form room, panting hard. Mr Lam was sitting at his desk, marking books. Otherwise the room was empty. He looked up as she ran in, smiled and beckoned her over.

'Assembly,' he said quietly. 'I was excused today. Sit down, Abbi.'

Mr Lam carried on with his marking for a while, then he looked at her.

'Mum still not well?'

'No and I had to take Jordan again.'

'Has she been to the doctor?'

'Er ... well ... yes ... er ... I'm not sure...'

She was cross with herself. She wasn't putting on a very good show. She felt shaky and rather dizzy. She desperately hoped she wasn't going to faint.

The sound of many voices outside in the corridors saved Abbi from having to answer any more questions. It was time for Maths. Well, she had done the homework so Miss Cook would have no reason to pick on her this time. She stood up and shouldered her bag, manufactured a smile for Mr Lam and headed from the room.

Miss Cook was in a bad mood – when wasn't she? She thumped a heavy pile of books down on a boy's desk and ordered him to hand them out. Then she moaned for several minutes about why she was making the mistake of wasting her time trying to teach such a load of uncooperative, stupid brats.

For only a few seconds, she abruptly halted her hail of insults as she approached Will's desk at the back of the room.

'Well done, William Smith,' she said. 'At least we have one person who is intelligent and sensible amongst such an ignorant lot.'

'Thank you, Miss Cook,' said Will, grimacing up at her. 'It must be your excellent teaching.'

There were one or two gasps and a lot of open mouths.

Then, as Miss Cook marched away from him, Will stuck his tongue out. Abbi smiled.

'And what have you got to laugh about, Abigail Arnold?'

Abbi's smile vanished as the multi-decibels hit her ears.

'Nothing, Miss,' she mumbled, lowering her eyes. *Only you, you fat old fossil!*

'You're right there!' Miss Cook went on. 'Someone must have helped you with your homework.'

'No, Miss,' said Abbi. 'I did it myself.'

'Don't give me that! To get ninety-five per cent...'

Abbi saw red. She couldn't cope any more. It was all too much. This was the final straw. She glared up at Miss Cook.

'Leave me alone!' she cried. 'You pick on me for no reason and you don't even have the decency to admit it when I get my homework right. I told you I'd get it done, even the extra you gave me for no reason at all, and I did, without anyone's help, least of all yours!'

The room was alive with silence. Everyone seemed to be sprung, ready to take cover when the explosion came.

'Get out!' The shriek must have been heard all over town. 'Get down to the Head, this minute.'

Abbi grabbed her bag and slid from the room, red-faced and seething. She was livid with Miss Cook. That horrible woman had no right to talk to her like that. But she was even more angry with herself. She had really let herself down. Now there would be trouble with a capital T.

There was no way she was going to see Mrs Johnson. No. There was only one place she could go – home. She ran out of school. But when she got back, she had a dreadful shock. He was there again, Tony, that revolting, slimy drunkard of a stepfather. He staggered over to her as soon as she burst in the door and crushed her against him with his hairy arms. He stank of body odour and booze and his breath was like a sewer. She felt her flesh creep as his hands touched her.

'Hello, Abbi, my darling,' he slobbered, his foul spit splashing her face. 'Give your old dad a big kiss.'

Like a cornered animal, Abbi fought him off.

'You're not my dad!' she screamed. 'My dad was nothing like you. I hate you, you evil monster!'

As she escaped from the flat, she caught a glimpse of a polythene bag full of bottles and Mum draped across the sofa, her hair and clothes in a mess. In that moment, Abbi saw the expression in Mum's eyes. It was something like guilt mixed with a cry for help.

'Abbi!' she called as Abbi slammed the door, but there was no way Abbi was going back in, not while he was there.

Abbi wandered the streets, searching for somewhere to hide. In the end, she sat on a bench in the park for hours, desperately trying to work out what she could do.

She didn't think she would dare go to school again. The Head wouldn't let a fourteen-year-old girl get away with that.

It was best she didn't go to school any more. Then they couldn't get at her. She could run away, get a job. She could pass for sixteen. It would be all right.

But suddenly, she knew that it was impossible. She couldn't abandon Mum, however much she hated what she had become. Stick together, was what she had always determined that they must do, not run away. Then there was Jordan. She couldn't leave him either. He needed her.

It was three o'clock, time to fetch him from school. She just hoped he hadn't been in too many fights or caused too much trouble in the class.

She stood in a shady corner of the playground and watched the classroom door. After a while, she saw little children streaming out into the playground. Where was Jordan? She waited for several minutes, but there was no sign of him. She began to panic. Had she missed him? She stepped forward into the sunlight, heading for the classroom door, but before she could reach it, he was dashing out, like a whirlwind. His face was stormy as he charged into her, almost knocking her over.

'Where were you?' he demanded.

'Over there,' said Abbi, pointing and regaining her balance. 'What kept you?'

'My teacher won't let us out until we can see our carers,' said Jordan crossly. 'You weren't there until just now. Come on. I want to go home.'

Home! Abbi froze inside.

'I thought we could go to the park for a bit,' she said. Perhaps *he* would have gone by the time they had spent some time there.

'I don't want to go to the stupid park.' Jordan was shouting and stamping his feet. Everyone was looking. His teacher was standing at the classroom door, watching.

'All right,' hissed Abbi, feeling her face reddening. 'No park.'

Where else could she take him? She had no money so the shops were out of the question. But Jordan was racing ahead and after a few minutes, he reached the front door of the flats.

'Are you sure you wouldn't like to go to the park?' Abbi asked in a last desperate effort to stay away from Tony.

'Yeah.' Jordan dashed inside and began pressing the lift buttons and yelling at the silver doors. 'Come on, you stupid lift, hurry up.'

'OK,' said Abbi. She would have to suffer. 'By the way, your dad's here.'

'Oh.'

Jordan pulled a face and did the thumbs down sign. They stepped into the lift and Abbi felt the pressure in her feet as it rose rapidly to the ninth floor. She felt her stomach tighten as the lift stopped and they walked to the front door. Then she inserted her key in the lock and pushed open the door. Tony was still there.

'Hello, son!' he called. 'Come over here, you young horror, and tell your dad what you've been up to. Have they thrown you out of school yet?'

'No,' said Jordan indignantly. He picked up the TV zapper and pointed it at the television. Then he sat down on the floor and stared at the screen.

Abbi noticed that Mum was asleep on the sofa so she slipped to her bedroom. She couldn't bear to be anywhere near that man. But she soon found it was a mistake to try to hide away. She had hardly sat down at her table before she heard the light creak of the door and smelled the tell-tale reek. She whipped round to face Tony by the time he had entered the room.

'What do you want?' she demanded.

Tony was leering. She felt sick. How she had stood those two years when this revolting specimen had lived with them all the time she could not imagine.

'Just wanted to see how my beautiful stepdaughter was blossoming,' he said, his voice slurred with drink.

'I'm not beautiful and I'm certainly not blossoming,' snapped Abbi, standing up and dodging round him.

She escaped through the door and into the bathroom where she locked herself in. Half an hour later, feeling very hungry, she risked opening the door and crept along to the kitchen. Besides, it was time Jordan had something to eat, too, if she was to get him to bed at a reasonable hour. There was no sign of Tony. A shudder of relief travelled though her. He had gone.

Quickly, she prepared jam sandwiches as there was still nothing in the fridge, put the kettle on and hurried into the living room. Jordan was still glued to the TV and Mum was still asleep. Abbi decided to risk waking her. She gently shook her arm and called close to her ear.

'Mum, wake up. I'll make you a black coffee, shall I?'

Mum stirred, opened her eyes, groaned and sat up.

'What time is it?'

Abbi flared up.

'Time you stopped seeing that man!' she snapped. 'Why did you go letting him in here again? You know he's nothing but trouble.'

'I know,' said Abbi's mum. Her voice was slow. She seemed twenty years older again this evening. 'I went out this morning and there he was. I'm sorry Abbi, but it's always the same. I can't say no. He always manages to sweet talk his way back in...'

As she spoke, Abbi heard a key in the lock.

'You've got to get rid of him,' she whispered in Mum's ear.

Mum nodded. 'OK,' she said. 'I will.'

Chapter Six

First thing next morning, Abbi was awake and sitting up in bed. She had hardly slept even though she had barricaded the door with her desk and a couple of chairs. Tony had persuaded Mum that he was staying overnight. There was no way Abbi was going to risk him arriving in the middle of the night, thank you. She had tasted a big enough hint of his lecherous ways that afternoon.

But, in spite of lack of sleep, she was feeling alert, her brain on overdrive. First, there was that evil man. He had to go.

Second, she knew she was going to have to speak to someone. She couldn't cope alone any more. But who could she trust? She had seen adverts for Childline. Maybe she could ring them. She didn't have to say her name, just ask for advice.

But third, school – what was she going to do about that? If she went in, she would have to face the Head. If she didn't go in, the Head would report her absence. Someone would be round to the flat. Then, who knows what would happen.

While Abbi dressed and got Jordan ready for school, she weighed up the school situation. Eventually, she decided it would be best to go in. Maybe she could breeze in as if nothing had happened. Or maybe she should talk to Mr Lam.

The class was still in registration with Mr Lam when she arrived. She was aware of everyone staring at her, even though she had tried to slip in unnoticed, and she heard whispers and sniggers. She glanced at Mr Lam as she sat down and he nodded and marked her in the register.

'You've had it now!' hissed Charlie.

Abbi tried to ignore her.

'She found out you skipped out of school,' whispered Grace.

'She's after your guts,' said Ellie, sounding as if she was delighted about it.

Mr Lam stood up and walked towards the door.

'Abbi,' he said quietly and beckoned.

She followed him, feeling all the energy draining out of her legs.

'Mrs Johnson sent for me,' said Mr Lam as soon as they were in the corridor away from the classroom door.

Abbi felt dizzy and leaned on the wall for support. She had known this was coming. She had heard about what happened to people who had to see the Head. Some of them had been suspended or expelled.

'She had had a complaint from Miss Cook,' said Mr Lam. 'Why didn't you go and see Mrs Johnson yesterday when Miss Cook sent you?'

'I don't know,' Abbi muttered. 'I panicked.'

'And you ran home?'

Abbi nodded.

'Well, you'll be pleased to hear that Mrs Johnson has asked me to deal with this,' said Mr Lam.

Abbi shuddered. Well, that was one ordeal she wouldn't have to go through.

'Abbi, you must realise you can't talk like that to staff.'

'I know, but—'

'I confided in Mrs Johnson,' he went on, 'that I feel that you are under some sort of stress, not only at school, but, well, you haven't been able to talk frankly to me, and, as I said before, I wish you would talk to someone.'

Abbi felt the tears welling up, but fought them back. She nodded. He had saved her from a visit to the Head and he wasn't like that other teacher who had let her down. It was time to trust him.

'I'm afraid of people coming and splitting us up,' she whispered.

'Who's us?'

'Me and Jordan, that's my little brother, and Mum.'

'But why would anyone want to do that?'

'I can't tell you.'

'Abbi…'

'Please don't make me.'

'So you have to look after the family?'

Abbi nodded, but sudden doubts shot into her brain. Had she hinted too much?

'I don't want to say any more,' she said.

'Fair enough,' he said. 'But you know I'm here if you need me.'

Throughout the day, Abbi managed to keep away from Charlie and her friends so they didn't harass her. She avoided Will when she found herself in his group for one subject or another. She couldn't handle any more comments from him. She was on edge all day, but the time passed by and before she knew it she was running to fetch Jordan from school. Jordan was like a roaring thundercloud rolling round the classroom by the time she picked him up, at least half an hour late.

'You must be Abbi,' said his teacher as she ran panting in the door. 'I'm Miss Mason.'

Abbi nodded, trying to hold off Jordan's punches.

'Jordan talks about you a lot,' said Miss Mason.

'I don't!' yelled Jordan. 'I hate her.'

Jordan lashed out at Abbi. Abbi gripped both his wrists hard.

'Hey, careful, Abbi!' Miss Mason looked shocked.

'OW!' Jordan screamed, wriggling and kicking. 'You're hurting me!'

Abbi felt bad, but she had to stop him somehow. He had hurt her, too. She kept hold of him and waited for him to calm down.

'We kept ringing your home number,' said the teacher, 'but there was no reply.'

'Ah,' said Abbi. 'Well, thanks for looking after Jordan. I came as soon as I could.'

'Your parents,' began the teacher.

'My mum's not well,' Abbi blurted out before she could go on. 'And Jordan's dad doesn't live with us any more.'

'He does,' argued Jordan. 'He came in last night and—'

'Well yes,' Abbi said, warning Jordan with her eyes. 'He does pop in from time to time, but he—'

'I understand,' said the teacher. 'Well, when your mum's feeling better, I need to have a word with her.'

'OK,' said Abbi. 'I'll tell her.'

Abbi couldn't get out of there quickly enough. She kept a tight hold of one of Jordan's hands and dashed out of the door.

I seem to be running away all the time, she thought as they hurried home, *escaping from one problem, only to run into another.*

That was certainly true. As she and Jordan entered the flat, the smell of booze nearly knocked her over and the sound of Tony's drunken laughter belted out from the living room. Mum hadn't kept her promise to get rid of him.

Abbi couldn't bring Jordan into this.

'Wait here,' she whispered, leaving him at the door. She put her finger to her lips and winked. He nodded. Luckily, his mood had swung back and he seemed to be remembering their secret.

Abbi tiptoed along to her room and found her old piggy bank. She guessed there was hardly any money in it, but it would be enough to buy them something to eat. She ran back to Jordan with a handful of coins.

'Come on,' she whispered. 'Quick, before he notices us.'

'Where are we going?'

'Out!'

Abbi hardly breathed until they were outside the flats.

'A treat,' she said. 'Where shall we go?'

'McDonald's!'

There was just enough money to fill them both up, though Abbi would have loved a thick creamy milkshake. It was almost dark before she summoned up enough courage to take her brother home. They couldn't stay out all night.

Neither Mum nor Tony noticed them come in, so Abbi went through the routine of putting Jordan to bed and then sitting down to her homework, but her mind kept wandering.

Then she remembered. She had no clean clothes. She needed to go upstairs to the washing room on the eleventh floor and put a load in. There were five washing machines and three dryers up there, shared by all the residents in the flats. She hoped one of the washers would be free.

She gathered as many of her own and Jordan's clothes as she could find and headed up two flights of stairs. But she had just clicked the machine door shut and pressed the start button when Tony staggered in. His shirt was grimy and unbuttoned halfway down and he was sweating heavily. He had a determined look in his bleary eyes and this time, Abbi somehow knew it was going to be more difficult to get away from him.

'Caught up with you at last,' Tony spluttered as he made a lunge in Abbi's direction. 'Where've you been hiding all day?'

'Out!'

Abbi dodged away, but Tony was too quick.

'Come on, my sweet,' he said as Abbi backed into a corner. 'Give us a kiss.'

Abbi gritted her teeth and tried not to look at this revolting specimen, but he was so close that he blocked her vision. Now she was seriously scared. How was she going to stop him? She had more than suspected his intentions on several occasions, but now it was obvious. He was so big and strong, she would never be able to keep him off. But she would fight.

Quickly, she swung her arm behind her and brought it round hard so her closed fist landed in Tony's eye. He roared and swayed drunkenly, but he didn't back off. In fact, he seemed more determined than ever to have what he wanted from her. His hands roughly grabbed at her and he began pulling at her clothes.

'Right, you little madam,' he spat in her ear. 'You'll pay for that.'

She wanted to be sick. She felt weak-kneed all of a sudden and her head was reeling. She opened her mouth and screamed, but the washing machine was making such a din, she wondered if anyone would hear. Almost immediately, though, her scream was deadened by Tony's foul mouth closing on hers. She bit his lip hard.

'Ah!' he yelled, but he didn't release his grip on her.

Then she went berserk, desperately scratching and biting and punching. Somehow, she wrenched herself away and slid down, out of his grasp. She screamed again.

Suddenly, the door opened and their neighbour from upstairs stepped into the room.

'Everything all right?' he asked.

Abbi could have laughed if she hadn't been so petrified. What a question!

'N-no,' she stuttered.

Tony pushed past the neighbour and shot out of the door.

'I was—' said the neighbour, '— got my washing, but...'

Abbi struggled to her feet.

'This machine's empty,' she said, trying to control the shakes in her voice.

'Oh, right.'

Abbi had never really spoken to this man before, but she was so glad to see him. She sat down on the floor opposite the machines, trembling from head to toe, and watched the neighbour set his machine off. Then she stared at both lots of washing going round and round. She felt like a zombie.

'That bloke?' asked the neighbour, sitting down on the window-sill and opening a book.

'My stepfather,' said Abbi.

'Ah,' said the neighbour. Then he began to read.

Abbi was tempted to tell this stranger what had happened, but decided against it. What would he do? It was none of his business. He wouldn't be interested. She didn't feel like talking, anyway. She just wanted to curl up and hope it would all go away.

Slowly, the trembling stopped. The machine finished its cycle and Abbi stuffed the clothes into a dryer. After half an hour, she took the hot clothes from the dryer and folded them. It made her feel much better, doing something totally boring like that. Then she nodded to the neighbour and left the room. The next hurdle was to get back into the flat and to her room safely.

Relief spread like a warm wave over her when she discovered Tony snoring very loudly on the settee. He had several scratches on his face, a fat lip and a red ring round one eye. Good, he'd get more than that if he dared come near her again. She tiptoed past the sitting room, peeped in Mum's room to check that Mum was fast asleep there and made for her own room.

The light was on and Jordan was sleeping deeply. She barricaded the door again and sat down to her homework. It was nearly ten o'clock.

When Abbi nervously emerged from her room at seven the next morning, she met Tony outside the bathroom and her stomach lurched sickeningly. But he acted as if nothing had happened between them and only offered her a filthy look. She hurried on with her daily routine, frightened that he would suddenly attack her. When Jordan woke up, she felt a little safer.

'I'll take him to school,' said Tony as Abbi made her brother's jam sandwich.

'No.'

'Why not? He's my son. I have every right.'

'I—' She didn't trust Tony to take Jordan, but at least it meant that she would be able to get to her own school on time. That was one problem less. 'OK.'

She made a cup of tea for Mum and found her awake, sitting up on the bed.

'Oh, Abbi,' groaned Mum. 'I'm sorry. There's you looking after me again. I'll make it up to you, really I will.'

'You broke your promise yesterday,' Abbi whispered as she passed the cup into shaking hands. 'You said you'd get rid of him.'

'I know – it's not that easy, Abbi. I—'

'Get him out of here, that's all!'

Mum nodded. She probably hadn't seen the scratches on Tony's face yet. She wouldn't know what he had attempted last night. She might not believe it anyway if Abbi told her and he would deny everything, of course.

'Yeah,' she said. 'He's bad news.'

'Will you be able to meet Jordan this afternoon?' Abbi asked.

'Yeah,' said Mum again.

Abbi ran from the flats. There was plenty of time before school, but she had made up her mind. She was going to ring Childline. She found a phone box and lifted the receiver.

'Hello,' she said when a man answered. 'I think I need help.'

Chapter Seven

'Hello, Childline.' The man's voice sounded kind.

Abbi gulped, feeling tongue-tied.

'I'm John,' said the voice. 'Can I help you?'

'It's my mum,' said Abbi, feeling instantly guilty. Was she was betraying Mum? 'She's got a problem.'

'Would you like to tell me about it?' said John.

'I don't want to let her down.'

'You won't be doing that,' said John. 'In fact, just the opposite. You're trying to help her, aren't you?'

'Yes, I suppose so, but I don't want her to know, nor anyone else.'

As soon as she had received a promise from John that the phone call was totally confidential, she began pouring out her problems. She talked for a few minutes and John listened, making a few comments to encourage her.

'You've done exactly the right thing, phoning us,' said John when Abbi stopped. 'Now I'm going to give you the number of a special group who can help with your problem. It's the National Association for the Children of Alcoholics. Have you got a pen?'

Abbi wrote down the number.

'Thanks,' she said then rang off and hurried along to school.

Abbi worried all day. Her brain was bombarded by hundreds of questions. She shouldn't have made that call. She wasn't sure if John would keep everything secret as he had promised, or whether she could trust him. She wondered if Jordan was all right. Did he get to school safely? She hoped Mum would pick him up on time and that she had finally got rid of Tony. If not, how was she going to survive another evening with him around? And it was only a matter of time before both schools would start asking serious questions.

She was so deep in these thoughts that she forgot to be on her guard. She was slowly drifting along to first period, Biology, when she felt a hand on her arm and her whole body jarred as if she had been touched by an electrical force. Her heart was racing as she whipped round.

'Hands off!' she exploded.

'Hey!' Will stepped back, his hands in the air, palms towards her. 'Chill out, Abbi.'

Abbi shuddered with relief.

'Oh, it's you,' she said. 'You made me jump.'

61

'Sorry,' said Will. 'Only you look so miserable lately. I thought there might be something up with you, that's all.'

Abbi looked at Will. Did he really mean it? She couldn't believe him. He was so good looking. Why should he waste his time?

'Straight up,' he said. 'If you need help...'

Then he shot ahead and ran into the Biology lab, shoving three other boys out of the way and making them laugh with some joke or other. No, Will was not to be trusted, any more than the rest of them.

But at break, Abbi wished for an ally when she saw Charlie and Ellie walking towards her. She doubled back.

'Creep!' called Charlie. 'Fancy getting ninety-five per cent in Maths.'

Abbi escaped through a flowerbed. She was in such a hurry that she dropped her Maths book in the mud. She heard Charlie and Ellie laughing as she picked it up, then she dodged into a side door of the school. But she couldn't relax. It was Maths last lesson, with Miss Cook. She hadn't faced that old witch since her outburst. She was dreading it. If she skipped Maths, she could make that second phone call. Then she would still have time to pick up Jordan if Mum forgot.

But as Abbi sidled towards the school door just before the last period, she came across Miss Cook, who threw her a filthy look as she sailed past her.

'Right,' Miss Cook said. 'Books out! Work on board. Five minutes!'

Abbi opened her book and began the work, but she was aware of a deep shadow as Miss Cook came and stood behind her.

'I don't know how you dare show your face here,' she said.

'Sorry,' murmured Abbi, guessing an apology would do no good, but she had to try. 'I didn't mean—'

'Don't you try and be cocky with *me*,' said Miss Cook.

'I'm not.'

'Don't you argue with *me!*'

Suddenly, Miss Cook spotted the book.

'What have you been doing with…?'

'She threw it in a puddle,' interrupted Ellie.

'I—' Abbi could hardly speak.

'It was an accident.'

Everyone turned to the back of the room where Will was casually pushing his chair back on to two legs and resting his feet on his desk.

'Who spoke?' demanded Miss Cook.

'I did,' said Will, beaming across the room. 'I saw it happen.'

Miss Cook melted instantly.

'Oh, thank you, William. An accident, you say.' She smiled at him, then she turned back to Abbi. 'We'll forget about the book, but you need to be punished for not going to the Head when I sent you.'

'But I've seen Mr Lam.'

'You can have some more extra work.' Miss Cook found an exercise in the text book. 'In my pigeon hole again, tomorrow morning without fail.'

She turned and squeezed between the rows of desks and made for the front of the room. She pointed to the work written on the whiteboard. 'Right! As I said, five minutes.'

After two minutes, when Abbi had finished the work on the board, she began the extra work. By the time Miss Cook told them to stop working, she had done half of it. She stole a glance at Will. He caught her eye and winked. Abbi turned away quickly, feeling a deep hot blush spread across her face. But she didn't wait at the end of the lesson to find out why he had come to her aid again. As soon as the bell went, she snatched everything up from her desk and headed out.

It was four-thirty. Abbi and Mum were sitting together over a cup of tea while Jordan watched children's TV. Perhaps things weren't quite so bad after all.

One, her mum was sober.

Two, Mum had fetched Jordan from school.

Three, Jordan was in a good mood.

Four, Tony had gone.

'I've thrown Tony out,' Mum began. 'For good, this time.'

Abbi knew she should feel relieved, but she had heard so many promises before. Tony had always managed to wheedle his way back in.

'Did he really go for you?' Mum asked, but she didn't look Abbi in the eye. 'Was he trying to…?'

Abbi gripped her mug of tea, her nerves instantly on edge. She watched Mum light up.

'Why do you ask?' she asked.

'That nice man from upstairs called. Said he had walked in on something he didn't like the look of. Wanted to know if I was aware of what was going on.'

Abbi waited for Mum to go on.

'I confronted Tony straight away. He denied it, of course. He almost convinced me the man had been lying, but then I asked him about the marks on his face. He couldn't give me a satisfactory answer. Said he'd walked into a door, of all things. The oldest one in the book! So is it true?'

She turned at last to look at Abbi. Abbi nodded.

'Oh, God!' Mum cried, tears streaming. 'What a monster! I'm sorry.'

She put her arm round Abbi.

'It's OK, Mum.'

It wasn't OK, but Abbi would not let herself give in. She had to be strong. She had to see this through. She had to be practical. For instance, she knew that there was still no food in the flat and she wondered if it had occurred to Mum that they would be hungry.

'Shall I go out and get something for tea?' she asked as she put down her empty mug.

Mum seemed to start out of a dream.

'Oh, yes,' she said. 'Would you?'

Abbi leapt up.

'Got any money?' she asked.

Mum shook her head.

'No,' she said, 'but I'll give you my Post Office Book and you can draw the allowance.'

She hurried away and returned with the book, signed it and handed it to Abbi. Abbi let herself out of the flat, pleased that Mum had parted with the book. Mum sometimes let her do this. At least Abbi had some money from time to time.

As soon as she was handed the cash over the counter, Abbi made for the mini-market across the road. She bought all sorts of things they needed and a few they didn't. Then she had to stagger home with two heavy bags, but before she reached the flats she threw the mini-market receipt in a bin and slipped a five pound note into her pocket.

She felt terribly guilty – it was stealing from Mum, but it wasn't for herself, this secret supply of money. It was for emergencies.

'You spent how much?' Mum exclaimed, wide-eyed as Abbi unpacked the shopping.

Abbi repeated the figure and handed her mum what was left of the money.

'We needed to stock up a bit,' said Abbi. 'Jordan's only had jam sandwiches to eat lately.'

'Oh.' Her mum's face crumpled again. 'I hate myself for this,' she cried. 'I really do.'

Yes, Abbi thought, until the next time.

But she hugged her mum and they cooked tea together.

This was the sort of life she wanted, doing things together like they used to. She could just remember the times before Jordan was born, before Tony came along and ruined everything. If only…

Chapter Eight

Over the next week, Abbi struggled on, balancing her life between the problems of school on the one hand and the difficulties at home on the other.

That's what my life's going to be like from now on, she thought. *But I have to do it. I have to protect myself and Jordan and Mum.*

For a short while, Mum really did try hard. Abbi put off phoning the second charity because she couldn't help hoping that Mum had really kicked the habit, but her own troubles were not over at school.

She was always treading on thin ice with Miss Cook and she had to struggle from one confrontation with Charlie, Ellie and Grace to another. She hated them. They were spiteful and cruel. It seemed so unfair. They had everything they wanted and they had a great social life, while she had nothing. How she would have loved to give them an earful, a taste of their own medicine.

But it didn't last. One morning a letter arrived. Abbi saw Mum pick it up and open it. She watched Mum's expression change.

'It's from Tony!' cried Mum. 'He says he wants to try and prove I'm an unfit mother. The foul swine wants custody of Jordan. Never!'

That was the trigger to start Mum drinking again.

'Don't, Mum, please,' pleaded Abbi that evening as Mum opened her fourth can of beer. 'Can't you see? If you keep getting drunk, they might do it, we might lose Jordan.'

But Abbi's pleading didn't do any good. She couldn't understand why Mum had to do it, but Mum couldn't stop herself and soon she had slipped back into her old ways. So Abbi began to take money regularly from Mum's purse. It was only pennies at first, then bigger coins. Her mum didn't seem to notice, so she became braver and took notes. With the money, she bought food and other essentials for the flat. She even bought Jordan a new pair of trainers from a charity shop. Her mum didn't miss the money. She was drifting lower and lower into her problem.

So one afternoon, after Abbi had skipped last lesson so she could pick Jordan up from school, she made up her mind. She had to ring that number that Childline had given her. Jordan came roaring out of school in a foul mood, so she let him choose his favourite ice cream to keep him quiet for a bit then she took him along to the park. There was a public phone box nearby. She left Jordan in the recreation area and ran to the phone box. Quickly, she dialled the freephone number.

'National Association for Children of Alcoholics,' said a woman's voice. 'My name's Margaret. How can I help?'

'It's my mum,' Abbi began.

'Do you want to tell me about it, dear?'

Abbi could see that Jordan had finished his ice cream and was playing on the slide. While he was happy, she had a bit of time. Margaret listened for a while then she began asking questions.

'Do you find you are telling lies to cover up what's going on?'

'Yes,' Abbi confessed. 'All the time.'

'And how does that make you feel?'

'Bad.'

'Is there no other adult in your family you can turn to – your dad, a grandparent, someone like that?'

'No,' said Abbi. 'My real dad's dead and, well, it makes me feel sick to talk about my stepfather. He—' She paused. There was no point in going into that at the moment. 'The only other person is Nan.' She told Margaret about the rift with Nan.

'Oh, I see,' said Margaret, 'but you say you hear from her sometimes? Why don't you get in touch with her?'

'Because Mum's drinking was the cause of their split in a roundabout way,' said Abbi. 'I don't think Nan would be willing to help.'

'Don't be so sure,' said Margaret. 'Why not try, dear. Or is there nobody of your own age you can confide in?'

'No – except – no, nobody.' She had almost mentioned Will, but she didn't even know him and she still wasn't sure about him.

'And are you afraid to bring your friends home?'

'I haven't really got any friends.'

'I see,' Margaret said again. 'And have you thought of speaking to someone in social services?'

'I daren't,' said Abbi. 'I'm terrified they'll split us up.'

'That's not necessarily so,' said Margaret. 'They—'

'Isn't there anything else I can do?'

'Well...'

Suddenly, Abbi saw Jordan thump another boy and try to push him off the slide.

'I've got to go,' she said.

Jordan was swinging dangerously from a bar near the top of the slide. The other boy was crying and

71

his mum was comforting him, looking angrily at Jordan.

'Wait,' said Margaret. 'We should talk a bit more.'

'Sorry I can't,' said Abbi.

Abbi thumped the receiver down, grabbed everything and dashed towards the slide.

'Jordan!' she yelled. 'Don't be such an idiot!'

Jordan dropped to the ground and landed like a gymnast. Abbi let go of her bag and hugged him. He pushed her off, but he was grinning.

'Is that your brother?' demanded the other boy's mother.

Abbi nodded.

'Well, you'd better teach him not to be so rough.' She took the boy's hand. 'Come on, love,' she said to him and marched out of the playground.

'I'm a chimpanzee!' shouted Jordan. 'Watch me!'

Before Abbi could stop him, he had shinned up a rope ladder and was balancing along a high pole, making chimp noises. She held her breath until he reached the far end and leapt down to the ground safely.

'Come on,' she said. 'Time we were going home.'

But it was half an hour before she could drag him away from the park. In the end she had to bribe him with a promise of hot dogs for tea.

'Who did you phone?' Jordan asked as they waited for the lift.

'Oh, just a friend,' said Abbi.

The next day, Abbi found she could not escape early from school. Her only choice was to head for the last lesson where she fidgeted so much that Mr Scott, the history teacher, noticed.

'For heaven's sake, Abbi!' he exclaimed, stopping mid-sentence about which period of history Abbi had no idea. 'You're like a cat on hot bricks. What's the matter with you, eh?'

'Nothing,' Abbi mumbled.

Then Mr Scott went back to his ramblings. Abbi tried to listen, but soon found herself counting the minutes until the bell went.

'Right!' said Mr Scott at last.

Two minutes later, Abbi was like a hare out of a box, sprinting for the school gate, running down the road. There was no point in going to Jordan's school now. He must have left ages ago. She decided to hurry straight home. But when she arrived panting at the flat, there was no one there.

As soon as Abbi opened the door, she sensed it. The place felt silent and empty, but she still called and searched all the rooms, just in case. Where were they?

Was something wrong? She looked for a note, but there was no clue as to where they had gone.

There was no time to wait for the lift. She quickly ran back to the stairs and leapt two at a time down to the ground floor and ran out into the street. She would try the park first. As she dashed in the park gates, she scoured the playground for Jordan and Mum, but there was no sign of them. Abbi stood for a few minutes, wondering what to do next. She had a bad feeling about it. Something *was* wrong. She couldn't understand it. When Mum fetched Jordan from school they either went straight home or to the park. Where else could they be?

Suddenly, a lady hurried over to her. Abbi recognised her. It was one of the mums from Jordan's class.

'It *is* Jordan's sister, isn't it?' asked the mum.

A shiver passed through Abbi's body. Something was *definitely* wrong.

'What's happened?' she demanded, frightened.

'It's OK. Don't worry,' said the mum. 'It's just that I had a meeting with Miss Mason after school and by the time I left, Jordan was still there.'

'Oh, God! Thanks!'

Abbi left the park as quickly as she had entered it. In a couple of minutes, she reached Jordan's school and rushed towards the classroom door. Jordan left the building and hurtled towards her, yelling angrily.

'Where've you been? I've been waiting ages and ages. I hate you, Abbi. I really hate you.'

Jordan's words hurt Abbi terribly. It wasn't her fault. She was doing all she could, wasn't she? But poor little Jordan! It wasn't his fault either. Where was Mum?

Abbi would have taken Jordan straight home, but she was aware of two people bearing down on her. It was Jordan's teacher and a man she had seen once before. She guessed he was the headteacher.

'We'd like a word with you,' said the man. 'I'm Mr Hayward, the Head. And you know Miss Mason.'

Lamely, Abbi followed them inside, her brain in overdrive. What was she going to tell them? Jordan complained and cried, but finally he held Miss Mason's hand and came quietly. They went to the Head's office and sat down.

'Mum must have been delayed,' Abbi began, speaking very fast as her brain whirred. She sat on the edge of the chair and gripped her hands firmly together. 'She was going to London today. She must have been held up. Perhaps it's the trains.'

She saw Mr Hayward and Miss Mason glance at each other.

They don't believe me, she thought, but she had to carry on with her story.

'She had an appointment,' she gabbled. 'I expect she's almost home by now and she'll be worried about Jordan and me. We'd better be going. Come on, Jordan.'

She stood up.

'Abbi,' said Mr Hayward, as if he hadn't been listening to a word she said. 'How old are you?'

'Fifteen,' said Abbi. She didn't see any harm in lying about that.

'And which school do you go to?'

Abbi felt like a coiled spring, suddenly sharing her brother's anger.

'Why should I tell you?' she burst out. 'You have no right to ask me. I've done nothing wrong.'

'We're not saying you have,' said Miss Mason gently, 'but you must admit, this isn't the first time Jordan has had to wait to be picked up. We're concerned, that's all.'

'This appointment in London,' said Mr Hayward. 'Was it at a hospital? Is she ill?'

Abbi's head wanted to explode. She would tell this nosy parker what she thought of him. Then suddenly, she remembered her outburst to Miss Cook. Speaking her mind only caused more trouble. She bit her lip hard and clenched her fists, digging her finger nails into the palms of her hands.

'No,' she managed to say, hearing the strange juddering voice that came from her mouth. 'It was with a television company.'

Why she said that, she had no idea. It just slipped out.

'She's hoping for a small part on TV.'

'What?' shouted Jordan, who had been sitting sullenly in the corner all this while. 'Is Mum going to be on TV? But I thought you said—'

'I'll tell you about it later,' Abbi cut in.

It was a ridiculous story. She couldn't believe she had made up such a lot of drivel. And she knew Miss Mason and Mr Hayward wouldn't believe her either. It was too far-fetched. But Mr Hayward seemed to accept it.

'Oh,' he said. 'Well, good luck to her. But I want you to give her an important message from me.'

'OK,' said Abbi, stunned that he hadn't told her to stop telling him a pack of lies.

'I *must* see her tomorrow,' he said. 'And I mean *must*! Without fail! Will you give her that message, please? Anytime she likes, only it is vitally important.'

Abbi nodded. It looked like they were going to let her and Jordan go. That gave them a little more time.

She decided to say nothing more in case they changed their minds.

Miss Mason stood up and opened the door.

'I think you ought to know we have already spoken to the social services about your family,' said Mr Hayward kindly. 'They're already aware of some of your problems.'

Abbi froze. She didn't want social services to come checking up on them again.

'See you in the morning, Jordan,' said Miss Mason.

'Yeah,' said Jordan and ran from the room.

Abbi followed, feeling like a robot. That news had been such a bombshell.

'So what TV programme is she going to be on?' asked Jordan as soon as they were out of school.

Abbi stopped, pulled herself together, bent over and put her hands on his shoulders.

'No TV programme,' she admitted. 'Sorry, but I had to say something or they might not have let us go.'

Jordan grinned.

'Our secret,' he said. 'We couldn't tell them what she's really like, could we? But Abbi?'

'Yes?'

'Where *is* she?'

'I don't know.'

Abbi kept her fingers crossed all the way home, hoping that Mum would be there, but she wasn't and she didn't come home all evening either.

Chapter Nine

Abbi was desperately worried. It felt like someone was screwing up her guts. Something terrible must have happened.

She didn't want Jordan to worry so she made up a story about remembering that Mum had said she would be home late. Jordan seemed to take it all in. She must be very good at lying. She was getting so much practice lately. She turned the TV on and while he was watching his programmes, she picked up the phone book and found some numbers. But the local store had not seen her all day, nor had the pub.

Was Mum hurt? Had she had an accident? Could she be in hospital? Abbi looked up the local hospital number and dialled, but nobody of Mum's name or description had been admitted. She daren't phone the police – they might ask too many questions.

While Abbi's stomach churned on the inside, she tried to act as normal as possible. She gave Jordan his tea then read to him and put him to bed.

How could she concentrate on her homework? It was impossible. She spent the evening pacing like a tiger up and down the flat. Several times she was tempted to phone the charity, but chickened out each time. What could they do? She was fourteen. She was perfectly capable of looking after herself and Jordan.

But the worry about Mum nearly drove her mad. Had she met up with Tony and gone off with him? Abbi persuaded herself that Mum would never leave them, however much Tony tried to bully her. But if not that, where was she?

By three o'clock in the morning, she was desperate. Suddenly, she made up her mind. She had to do it. Mum might not be very pleased, but she would have to risk that. She picked up the receiver and dialled. A sleepy voice answered.

'Hello?'

'Hello, Nan,' Abbi whispered.

'Who's that?' Her nan sounded cross and half-asleep.

'It's Abbi, Nan, Lynn's daughter.'

'What's happened?' demanded Nan.

Abbi wished Nan could have said, 'How are you, dear?'
or 'I've missed you, Abbi.'

'It's Mum,' she whispered.

'What about her?' asked Nan.

'You don't happen to know where she is?' asked Abbi.

'Now, why on earth would I know *that*? You know
I haven't spoken to her for years. I washed my hands
of her a long while ago – when she took up with that
drunkard. I'm the last person to know where *she's*
got to.'

'Sorry, I—'

Abbi slammed the phone down and went along to the
bedroom. Jordan was fast asleep. She climbed up on to the
top bunk and tried to relax.

'Think of something nice,' Mum had always said when
she was little.

Eventually, she must have slept. As soon as she
opened her eyes and saw how bright it was, she knew
it must be late. She looked at the clock. It was nine
thirty. Too late to go to school now. Jordan was still
asleep.

Suddenly, she remembered. Mum? Was she home yet?
Abbi crept from the bedroom and along the corridor.
But Mum's room was exactly the same as the night
before, empty. Abbi lay down on the bed, buried her
head in the pillow and sobbed.

'Abbi!' Jordan called.

Quickly, Abbi dried her tears. She mustn't let her little brother see how worried she was. She must be strong, pretend she was in control. She met Jordan outside Mum's room.

'Where's Mum?' Jordan asked.

Abbi had to think on her feet.

'Oh, do you know, I am a silly forgetful person,' she said. 'She did say she might have to stay just one night away. I expect she'll be back any minute now.'

They ate breakfast. Jordan accepted Abbi's explanation. He was excited that he didn't have to go to school. But that fact brought on another worry for Abbi. She had promised that Mum would go to see Mr Hayward today. How could she, if she didn't know? How could Abbi tell her?

By the time they had finished breakfast, Abbi had made several phone calls, but the police and local hospital both said that they hadn't heard of Lynn French. She tried the local shops again and the pub, but no one knew where she was.

Next, they went to the park and while Jordan played on the equipment Abbi sat down to think. Who could she turn to now? She dare not call the social services, for obvious reasons. The only other option was ringing those charities again.

She was just about to go to the phone box when she heard someone calling her name. She whipped round. Will was jogging towards her. She wished the concrete would crack open so she could slip out of sight, but it was too late to do anything.

'Found you at last,' said Will, skidding to a halt.

'What...? Why – why aren't you at school?' Abbi stuttered.

Will grinned. 'I could ask you the same question,' he said. 'Actually, I went in this morning, but I skipped out at lunchtime.'

'Why?'

'When you weren't in school, Mr Lam started asking everyone if they had seen you. He was obviously concerned about you. Then Mrs Johnson came breezing in and they had a little huddle. I don't know if they have guessed what your problem is, Abbi, but I think the game's nearly up.'

'What do you mean?'

Before Will could answer, Jordan swung down from the top of the climbing frame.

'Who's that?' he shouted.

'His name's Will,' said Abbi.

'Is he your boyfriend?' asked Jordan.

'No, silly,' said Abbi, feeling the colour rising to her face.

Jordan made gorilla noises, pulled a face at Will and leapt back into action.

'Sorry about Jordan,' said Abbi. She suddenly thought of an excuse. 'I couldn't come to school. Jordan's not well.'

'He looks OK to me,' said Will. 'I don't think that will convince anyone.'

Abbi swallowed hard and looked at Will. Why had he risked getting into trouble for her?

'In case you're wondering, I think I've guessed what your problem is,' said Will.

'Problem?' Abbi tried to sound indignant. 'What problem?'

'Is it booze?' he said. 'Your mum?'

Abbi couldn't help bursting into tears. She felt Will's arm go round her shoulders and she felt like melting. It was time to tell all.

'Promise you won't breathe a word?' she began, wiping her eyes.

He nodded solemnly.

'OK.' Will removed his arm, but he sat quite close, ready to listen.

Abbi poured out the whole story, from the moment Tony appeared on the scene and ruined their lives.

'Apart from anything else,' she said, 'it's had a terrible effect on Jordan.'

'And you,' said Will.

'I've had to lie to everyone, including him, to keep things together, basically to keep Mum. I'm petrified of losing her. If we lose her, they might split us up.'

Will was nodding from time to time, encouraging her to go on.

'I know what you mean,' he said.

'You say the game's nearly up at school?' said Abbi. 'Well, it's the same at Jordan's school. They've told the social services.'

'So where's your mum now?' asked Will.

'I don't know.' Abbi dissolved in tears again. Will put his hand on her arm.

'Have you tried the hospital?' he asked.

'Yes,' said Abbi. 'Twice. And as many other places I could think of. I'm at my wit's end.'

She looked at her watch.

'I must go,' she said. 'I'm going to try the hospital again.'

'Good idea.'

'Time to go, Jordan,' she called.

'No!' yelled Jordan from the seesaw. 'I'm not coming!'

'Yes,' said Abbi, standing up.

Will stood up beside her. He seemed even taller than usual.

'I'd come with you,' he said. 'But I'd better head back to school before they miss me. Sorry.'

'That's OK.'

Abbi watched him go. She felt a little better than she had an hour before. It was great to have a friend. A trouble shared and all that.

Eventually, Abbi bribed Jordan off the seesaw and they hurried home. She was impatient to check whether Mum had returned while they were out. If there was still no sign of her, she would ring the hospital again. Then maybe she should try Nan.

Jordan was eating a chocolate bar they bought at the newsagents and was chatting happily with his mouth full as they went up in the lift and arrived at the flat. But Abbi couldn't relax. Her hands shook as she fumbled with her key and pushed it in the lock.

'Mum!' she called as she opened the door, but the flat had that same empty feeling she had experienced the day before. Mum wasn't at home.

'I need the toilet,' said Jordan.

'All right,' said Abbi.

She rang the hospital but the answer was the same. No Mum.

Where *is* she? Oh God, where is she?

Abbi was going frantic. She scoured the phone book. Who else could she ring? What could she do? She couldn't just sit here and wait. She had to do

something! Then she had an idea. She and Jordan
would go to the hospital and check. Just in case.

'Hurry up,' she called.

'Why?'

'We're going out again.'

'Oh no,' shouted Jordan. 'I want to watch TV. My
favourite programme's on. I've been waiting all week
for it.'

Jordan took forever in the toilet then he had to make
extra sure his hands were washed and dried properly.
Abbi was certain he was playing for time. She paced up
and down outside the bathroom.

'Come on!' she called several times.

She could throttle him sometimes! If only she could
have had a placid little brother who did as he was told.
Still, he wouldn't be Jordan if he was like that. And it
was Jordan she was trying to protect.

Fifteen minutes had passed. She had to think of
something to persuade Jordan that they had to go
out again.

'You know our little secret about Mum?' she called.

'What about it?' Jordan was grumpy, but at least he
was willing to talk.

'Well,' said Abbi. 'I'm worried about her. She should
have been home by now. So we have to search for her.
It's like she's lost in the jungle and—'

Luckily, she had hit just the right note. Jordan opened the bathroom door. He began racing up and down the corridor.

'—and we are the Rescue Rangers and we have to find her,' he said. 'OK. I'll be Ben the Brave. You can be Max the Mighty.'

Abbi couldn't help smiling at Jordan in spite of herself.

'Come on, then, Ben the Brave,' she said. 'Let's roll!'

She opened the door. A young lady and a bald man with a moustache were standing outside the flat. The young lady smiled at Abbi.

'Hello,' she said. 'You must be Abbi and this must be Jordan.'

'No,' said Jordan. 'I'm Ben the Brave and this is Max the Mighty, and we're Rescue Rangers.'

'I see,' said the young lady. 'And who are you going to rescue today?'

'Our mum!' said Ben the Brave proudly.

But Abbi was looking at the ID they were both showing.

'My name's Tanya,' the young lady was saying. 'I'm what you call a social worker. And this is DS Manning.'

With one swift movement, Abbi grabbed Jordan's arm, swivelled him round and shoved him back inside the flat. Then she followed him and slammed the door.

'Go away!' she yelled at the closed door. 'We don't want you here.'

Chapter Ten

'What did you go and do that for?' yelled Jordan, struggling with Abbi, trying to reach the door.

Abbi had to stop him. She said the first thing that came into her head.

'Those people,' she whispered. 'They've come to take us away. We'll have to go and live somewhere else. Then we won't be with Mum.'

Jordan was staring at her with wide eyes and a very pale face. Immediately, she regretted saying that. Why had she frightened him? Probably because she was so terrified herself.

There was a knock at the front door. Abbi felt her heart hit her ribs and Jordan clung to her.

'Abbi, open the door, will you?' called Tanya. 'We need to talk.'

'Go away!' Abbi shouted. She took Jordan's hand and pulled him into the sitting room. 'Look,' she said quietly. 'Sorry, don't be scared. It's not as bad as all that, really it isn't, but – let's put the TV on, shall we? You can watch that programme, can't you?'

Jordan zapped on the TV. He sat on the floor in front of it and stared at the screen. Abbi tried to ignore Tanya knocking and calling from outside the flat. She sat down on the sofa and tried to think. The schools must have contacted social services when she and Jordan hadn't turned up for school today.

The knocking continued, but she blocked it out. She had to think – think about what to do.

'Abbi!' called Tanya through the door. 'Please open the door. You know it makes sense. You're only making matters worse by locking yourselves in there. I need to talk to you about your mum. She's—'

Abbi put her hands over her ears. It was a trap. That mention of Mum.

She went into her bedroom and closed the door. That way she could hardly hear the knocking or Tanya's voice. But after a while, Abbi thought she should go and see if Jordan was all right. She opened the bedroom door and began to walk along the corridor. The knocking had stopped. Perhaps Tanya and the police officer had gone away.

But suddenly, as Abbi walked into the sitting room, she had the shock of her life. Tanya and DC Manning were sitting on the sofa, smiling up at her.

'How…?' Abbi began.

'Jordan let us in,' said Tanya, standing up. 'When you failed to answer me, I called him. He's a good boy, aren't you, Ben the Brave?'

Jordan turned away from the TV for a second and nodded and smiled.

'You had no right!' Abbi shouted. 'Taking advantage of him. He's only five.'

'I know,' said Tanya, holding out her hand towards Abbi. 'That's one reason we're here.'

Abbi stepped back.

'Well, at least sit down,' said Tanya. 'And listen to what I've got to say. That can't do any harm, can it?'

'No more than is done already,' snapped Abbi and she walked across the room and sat down. She looked around, suddenly embarrassed by all the empty bottles she hadn't had time to clear away.

'Abbi,' Tanya began again. 'I really admire your strength. You're a good loyal daughter and sister, protecting your mum and Jordan like this.'

'What do you mean?'

'Your mum has had a problem for some time. We have your family on our 'at risk' register.'

Abbi huddled in the chair and wrapped her arms round her knees. She felt like giving up. There was no point in denying everything any more.

'I suppose our schools blew the whistle on us,' she said. 'Did they ring you today because we weren't in school?'

'No, we're here for another reason. I'm sorry, Abbi, I have to be blunt. Your mum's an alcoholic, isn't she? She's ill and needs help.'

Abbi shivered, suddenly feeling icy cold.

'We don't know where she is,' she cried. She turned to DC Manning. 'I'm desperate. Can you help us find her? Please!'

DC Manning nodded.

'We've found her,' he said. 'She's the one who sent us round here.'

Abbi felt a kind of explosion inside her head. It was relief and pain and fear all rolled into one. She felt short of breath and dizzy. It was all over. She couldn't fight any more.

'Mum?' she said weakly. 'Where is she?'

'She's in hospital,' said Tanya. 'Now, don't worry, she's all right.'

But Jordan had heard what she said.

'Hospital?' he cried. 'I want to see her. I want my mum.'

He began to wail loudly. Abbi reached for him and pulled him on to her knee. Tanya zapped the TV off.

'The hospital?' shouted Abbi, suddenly angry. 'But I've been ringing and ringing. They said Mum wasn't there.'

'Did you phone the local one?' asked DC Manning.

'Yes.'

'They're right. She's not in there. She was taken by ambulance to the Emergency Department at the big hospital over the other side of the county.'

So that would explain it.

'Did she have an accident?' asked Abbi. 'What is it? A broken leg? Her appendix?' But she knew.

'None of those things,' said Tanya.

'Why didn't someone tell us before?' demanded Abbi as she regained some of her strength. 'I've been sick with worry. We had no idea where she was.'

'OK, calm down,' said Tanya. 'And I'll tell you what happened.'

Jordan was still crying with his face buried in Abbi's shoulder, but he was much quieter now and Abbi rocked him in her arms as she listened.

'Yesterday lunchtime, a woman was found lying at the side of the river several miles away,' said Tanya. 'She was unconscious.'

'Yesterday?' shouted Abbi. 'And you didn't tell us?'

'No,' said Tanya. 'I said '*a woman*' had been found. Nobody knew who she was. Tests found that the alcohol level in her blood was dangerously high. Basically, she was poisoning her system. So she was treated and kept under close observation. She was unconscious for almost twenty-four hours.'

Abbi gasped. All that time?

'She came round this morning, and the first thing she said was, "Abbi".'

Tears streamed down Abbi's face.

'I want to see her,' she cried.

'We'll see about that soon,' said Tanya. 'But she's still very ill.'

'But she needs us.'

'Of course she does.'

'What did Mum tell you?'

'I haven't seen her, but she told the nurses about you and Jordan and about the sad split with her mother. Then she wanted to get straight up and leave the hospital. She was anxious that she should go and meet Jordan from school. She's very confused. She didn't realise, of course, that she had missed a whole day. Then she gave her name and address and the hospital got on to us.'

'Sorry I was so mad at you,' said Abbi. 'You were right. I needed to protect Jordan. And I still do.'

'We need to find you a nice foster home.'

'No!' cried Abbi. 'We're OK as we are. I can look after Jordan. I've been looking after him and Mum for ages.'

'I'm sorry, Abbi. I know you have. That's what I admire so much about you, and if Jordan was older it might be different, but as he's only five—'

'You won't separate us. *Never!*' Abbi clutched Jordan hard. 'If we can't stick together, we won't go. I'll—'

'You'll be together, I promise,' said Tanya. 'We have several really kind people on our lists who would love to look after you for a while. Now what you need to do is pack a few things to take with you. Can I use your phone?'

Abbi nodded. Then, moving like a zombie, she found a suitcase and took it to the bedroom. She packed all the clean clothes she could find for both of them as well as Jordan's favourite toys, her clock and a few books. She shouldered her school bag, though she didn't know what was going to happen about school. How far away would this foster home be?

'When can we see Mum?' Abbi asked when she had finished.

'Tomorrow,' said Tanya. 'She really isn't strong enough to see you today. Anyway, I've made a few calls and found some people who'd love to welcome you into their home. Mr and Mrs Peters. They're a lovely couple. They've looked after loads of children over the years.'

Abbi shrugged her shoulders. One foster home was like any other, she presumed. As long as they didn't try to split her up from Jordan.

Tanya drove Abbi and Jordan to the Peters' house. It was about five miles away in a small town with a river and a lot of old buildings. Luckily, Jordan had switched moods again. He stared out of the window and chatted excitedly all the way. This was like an adventure for him.

Abbi was glad he could feel like that. She wished she could. But she found it impossible to stop shivering although it was quite a warm day. Her body felt tense and she was getting a headache. What would these people be like? Would they keep their promise to take them to visit Mum tomorrow? Where would all this end?

But Tanya was right. Mr and Mrs Peters were cheerful and kind.

'You must call us Ma and Pa,' said Mrs Peters as she took Abbi and Jordan upstairs. 'Everybody does. You don't mind sharing, do you? Brothers and sisters usually like to stick together.'

The taut muscles in Abbi's shoulders began to relax and the headache eased. Mrs Peters, Ma, seemed to understand how she was feeling.

There were bunks in the room, similar to those at home.

'I bags the top!' Jordan shouted, leaping up the ladder and diving onto the pillow.

Abbi shrugged.

'OK,' she said. She really didn't care either way. It was just a place to sleep for a night or two, until Mum came home.

They went back downstairs and Tanya prepared to leave.

'Now, don't worry about anything,' she whispered to Abbi. 'I'm working on your case. I'll do all I can to sort it out for you. And here's my number if you need anything.'

'Thanks,' said Abbi. Then she watched her drive away.

Chapter Eleven

As promised, Ma Peters took Abbi and Jordan to the hospital the next afternoon. Abbi had been amazed how well she had slept and Ma had made them feel so welcome that the morning passed quite quickly. Even Jordan played quietly with the toys Ma found for him. Abbi wondered if he was as nervous of going to see Mum as she was.

'Shall we take her some flowers?' Ma suggested and she helped Abbi pick a bunch from the garden.

At lunchtime, there was a phone call from the hospital. Could they go via the flat and fetch some of Mum's clothes?

I hope that means she's coming home today, thought Abbi.

The flat seemed even more hollow and empty than before. It was almost like they had been away for weeks instead of just one night. Abbi hurried to her mum's room and found some underwear, a blouse and jeans, a sweater, socks and a pair of trainers. She stuffed them quickly into a bag with Mum's nightie and dressing gown, her sponge bag and make-up and hurried back to Ma and Jordan, who were waiting in the sitting room.

'Nice flat,' said Ma, beaming at Abbi.

Abbi blushed.

'It needs tidying,' she said, hoping Ma had not spotted the bottles and cans.

Jordan had collected a few more of his toys.

'Is it worth taking those?' asked Abbi. 'We'll be back here in a day or two.'

'Don't be too optimistic about that,' said Ma.

Abbi's stomach lurched.

'What do you mean?' she demanded.

'Well, dear, it might take a little longer than just a day or two,' said Ma. 'Not long, mind, but – come on, I bet you can't wait to see her.'

Abbi was very quiet for the rest of the journey. She clutched the bunch of flowers and sniffed their faint perfume. What had Ma meant? Had she let something slip out? Did she know something?

The hospital was enormous and very confusing with so many corridors and lifts and reception desks and arrows pointing to various departments with such long names she couldn't pronounce them.

Ma seemed to know her way round, though, and took them up in a lift to the tenth floor. They followed signs to Princess Ward and suddenly, there was Mum, sitting up in bed in a plain white nightie, looking very pale.

'Mum!' yelled Jordan, running over and throwing himself at the bed.

Abbi dropped the bag of clothes and thrust the flowers at Ma. Then she dashed towards the bed and hugged Mum. Then she drew back, afraid to knock the tube fixed to the back of Mum's hand. She studied Mum's face. There was a cut over one eye and lots of bruising down one cheek. Then Abbi noticed the scratches and bruises on Mum's arms. She looked like she had been beaten up.

Jordan seemed stuck to Mum with glue, but Abbi gently held her hand and smiled.

'Missed you,' she said.

'Me, too. Abbi, I'm truly—'

Abbi put her finger over Mum's lips.

'Shh!' she whispered. 'Just get better, will you?'

She remembered Ma and the flowers. She turned round and beckoned to Ma who had stayed in the doorway. Abbi met her halfway.

'Mum,' she said as she took the flowers and held them out. 'These are for you. They're from Ma and Pa's garden. And this is Ma. We stayed at her house last night. And please, Mum, get better soon.'

She had gabbled it all out, fighting back the need to cry.

'Thanks. They're beautiful,' said Mum as she smiled weakly at Abbi. Then the smile faded. She looked up sadly. 'Hi,' she said to Ma, swallowing hard. 'Thanks for taking my kids in. I feel so ashamed...'

Abbi noticed her eyes glistening with tears.

'It's my pleasure,' said Ma. 'They're a delight.'

They stayed for almost an hour, by which time Jordan was showing signs of becoming bored. As Abbi fetched him down from bouncing on the empty bed next to Mum's for the hundredth time, she decided it was time to go. She would have liked to sit and talk with Mum all day, but it was impossible with such a hyperactive little brother.

'How long are they going to keep you in here?' she asked.

'They haven't said, but once I'm off this drip, I'll be out of here like a shot!'

Then what? wondered Abbi. *Will it be back to how it has been all these years?*

A nurse walked towards them. She smiled at Abbi.

'You must be Abbi,' she said. 'I've heard so much about you. The perfect daughter. You've got a very proud mum, you know.'

Warmth spread through Abbi and she felt like crying again. She grinned at Mum through watery eyes.

'Oh, she's just making it all up,' she said.

'And you're Jordan?'

Jordan stuck his tongue out then faced the other way. The nurse didn't seem to mind, but Abbi felt embarrassed.

'Jordan!' she complained.

'The doctor will be round soon,' said the nurse. 'He might give you some idea of when you can leave. He'll want to discuss your plans for the future.'

Abbi guessed what that meant. Mum was going to have to kick the habit and make promises that she would find hard to keep. Then, hopefully, their lives would change for the better.

By Monday, there was still no prospect of Mum leaving hospital. Abbi and Jordan had been to see her each day and Abbi was pleased that she looked better each time, but the nurse had indicated that it would be a little while yet.

It was an extremely nervous Abbi who stood waiting at the bus stop with Jordan and Ma early on Monday morning. She was terrified everyone would know. That the news would have reached her classmates via jungle telegraph. Or that it would be written all over her face in large letters – 'My mum's an alcoholic!'

At last the bus arrived and they squeezed on amongst loads of noisy school children of all ages. Abbi glanced around. Luckily, there was no one she knew, so she stared sightlessly out of the window until Ma nudged her back to the present. They were almost at her school. Abbi stood up, ruffled Jordan's hair, smiled at Ma and pushed her way off the bus.

'Keep your chin up!' called Ma.

'Yeah!' said Abbi, forcing a smile. Then she hurried towards school.

As soon as she entered the gate, she was convinced that everyone was staring at her.

'Hey!' she imagined them all whispering behind their hands. 'That's Abbi. Did you hear about her mum?'

She kept her head down and stood against the red brick of the old school building. After a moment, she saw Charlie by the gate and soon Ellie and Grace joined her. They hadn't noticed Abbi yet, but she knew it would be only a matter of time. Suddenly, someone was standing by her side.

'All right?' It was Will.

'Mmm,' she mumbled.

'Where were you on Friday?' Will asked. 'I went looking in the park again at lunchtime and after school, but you weren't there. Did you find your mum?'

Abbi felt a sigh of relief seep out of her. If Will didn't know then it was likely nobody did. Things might not be quite as dreadful as she thought. But why was he still so keen on keeping an eye on her? Then she remembered he hadn't told her how he guessed about Mum.

'Yes,' she answered. 'She's OK. But you never told me how—'

A loud bell sounded from inside school. Abbi was almost submerged in the solid stream of pupils pushing and shoving to get into school. Will was lost somewhere amongst them and she didn't see him again until she arrived in the form room a few minutes later. By then, Charlie, Grace and Ellie were sitting in their usual seats. Abbi went and sat down.

'Been ill?' whispered Ellie.

'Hangover, was it?' sneered Charlie.

Abbi didn't react. She wouldn't give them that satisfaction.

Mr Lam walked casually into the room.

'Morning,' he called with a grin. 'A good weekend had by all, I hope, and now we're all raring to go, eh?'

There was a chorus of groans around the class. He didn't say anything to Abbi. She assumed that he knew about what had happened in the last few days. Social services would have been in touch with school. He went through the routine of registration as normal, gave a few messages and answered a couple of questions.

But Abbi was filled with dread about first period. What a way to start a new week – Maths with Miss Cook.

On a nod from Mr Lam, there was the din of scraping chairs and chatter as everyone left the room. As Abbi slipped past Mr Lam's chair, he whispered,

'Come and see me at break, Abbi.'

He surely *must* know! Everything! Now what was he going to say?

But Abbi had to put that question to the back of her mind as she faced the more urgent challenges of avoiding Charlie and her friends in the corridors and coping with the razor sharp tongue of Miss Cook.

She made the Maths room safely and crept to her normal place. Miss Cook stormed in as usual and slammed a great pile of exercise books onto her table.

But amazingly, the lesson flew by with no hassle from Miss Cook. What was going on? Abbi couldn't understand it. Then she twigged. Miss Cook was in the know about her circumstances, too. How many of the other staff had been told?

As Abbi left the Maths room unscathed at the end of the lesson, she felt Charlie at her side.

'Mighty suspicious!' hissed Charlie. 'How much did you pay her to start being nice to you?'

'Hey, Charlie.' Will had pushed his way between them. 'Great disco Saturday night! You're a fantastic dancer.'

Charlie giggled, but Abbi couldn't help smiling. Good old Will! He had done that to protect her. She hurried away. She had her appointment with Mr Lam to keep. She dreaded what he would have to say this time.

Chapter Twelve

'I knew there was something very wrong,' Mr Lam began quietly as soon as they were sitting down. 'Why didn't you tell me?'

'I was frightened,' Abbi admitted.

'What of?'

'That you'd tell on me.'

'Tell on you?'

'So we'd be split up.'

'Well, you *are* split up now, aren't you?'

'Only for a few days, and Jordan and me are together and Mum will be out of hospital soon.'

'Yes, that's great. And hopefully she'll get the right kind of help. But school – I – we – would have been much more sympathetic if we'd known...'

'I don't want your sympathy,' stormed Abbi.

'I don't mean that. I mean we could have been supportive, as I hope we can be now.'

'So how many people are in the know? Miss Cook...?'

'Yes, she's been told what Mrs Johnson and I thought was necessary, and so has the rest of the staff who teach you.'

Abbi survived the rest of the day in a mixture of shame and embarrassment. Not that any of the staff said anything, but it was just the fact that they knew. She was in such a confused state at the end of the afternoon that she forgot to avoid Ellie and Charlie, who appeared one on each side of her as she walked out of school.

'Come on, Abbi,' Ellie mocked in her ear. 'You're going to come clean with us. We can't have you keeping that secret a second longer.'

Abbi stifled an urge to scream. Then she fought off the mad desire to yell the truth into their faces, but outside the gate they met Ma and Jordan on their way to the bus stop. Relieved, Abbi hugged both of them. Charlie and Ellie hovered for a moment, staring at Ma with puzzled expressions in their eyes then they ran off down the road. It gave Abbi tremendous satisfaction that, for once, she had got the better of them.

Jordan was in a good mood. Abbi suspected it was Ma's cheerfulness that had a calming influence on him. He chatted away about his day at school, where everything seemed to have gone well for a change, but then his face suddenly crumpled into tears.

'I miss my mum,' he cried.

'Yes, love, I know you do,' said Ma, holding his hand. 'Abbi does, too.'

Abbi nodded and held Jordan's other hand until they reached the bus stop.

'So, you'll be pleased to hear about a lovely surprise I've arranged for you when we get home,' said Ma.

'Mum?' yelled Jordan, making everyone in the bus queue turn round.

'Not yet, but—'

Jordan threw himself at Ma.

'I want my mum!' he screamed.

'Shush, dear,' said Ma, holding him gently. 'Soon.'

The bus came along at that moment and Ma refused to say another word about it, even though both Abbi and Jordan pleaded with her. Abbi felt slightly faint as she boarded the bus. What was the lovely surprise?

The journey seemed to take forever, but eventually, they reached their stop and jumped off. Abbi was in such a hurry that Jordan and Ma were both out of breath trying to keep up with her. But when they arrived at the Peters' house, there was no one there. Abbi slumped weakly on to a chair. Jordan ran from room to room searching for the surprise.

'Hang on, dear,' said Ma, glancing at her watch. 'Two minutes or thereabouts – that's all you have to wait.'

She went to the front window and peered out. After about a minute, she waved and turned round to Abbi and beamed. Abbi rushed to the window as a car stopped outside. She watched two people climb out. One was Tanya, but she could not identify the other one at that distance. It wasn't Mum. Mum was taller than that. Who was it? There was something familiar about her.

Suddenly, she felt all of the colour drain from her face and she steadied herself by gripping the window-sill tightly.

'Nan?'

'Yes, dear, your nan,' said Ma. 'Come on, let's go and let them in.'

As Ma opened the front door, Abbi hung back, shy of meeting Nan, but also, remembering the late night phone call, afraid Nan would be annoyed with her. Jordan stood beside Abbi and frowned.

'Who's that?' he asked rudely.

Abbi took his hand and led him into the sitting room.

'It's our nan,' she said quietly. 'You remember, I've told you about her?'

Jordan nodded, still frowning.

'What does *she* want?'

'I don't know.'

The door opened and Ma brought Nan and Tanya into the room. They were all smiling. Abbi was less worried, but she refused to look at Nan. Suddenly Nan was standing right there in front of her.

'Abbi!' she said. 'There's so much to say, I don't know where to begin, apart from the usual grandmotherly things like, how much you've grown since I last saw you and how pretty you've become and I've missed you terribly.'

Abbi felt her resistance melting like butter, but she held back even though she was dying to admit she felt the same.

'And I have to offer you an apology, too,' added Nan. 'The other night – I wasn't really awake – I didn't realise what you were trying to say. I didn't understand what you've been through, what a support you've been to your mum.'

Abbi didn't know how she found herself in her Nan's arms, but she knew it felt so good. There was that faint perfume smell and the softness of the bosom that brought back so much of her childhood in a flash. It was as if she had been waiting for this moment for years.

'Nan,' she murmured and closed her eyes to soak it all in.

But a light touch on her side reminded her of her responsibility, Jordan. She gently pushed away from Nan and turned to her little brother, who stood gaping, totally confused and worried, up at her. She crouched down beside him then lifted him up in her arms. He clutched her tightly.

'So you're Jordan,' said Nan.

Jordan buried his face in Abbi's neck.

'Jordan,' Abbi whispered. 'This is our nan.'

'Why?'

'Because she's our mum's mum and that makes her our nan.'

'I'll make tea, shall I?' said Ma.

'Good idea,' said Tanya. 'I'll come and help.'

Jordan took a while to release his grip on Abbi, but the more she talked to him and explained everything as simply as she could, the looser his arms became round her neck. He stole several glances at Nan, who was sitting on the sofa, watching them. She didn't try to push herself on Jordan. It seemed she could wait. The tension lines in Jordan's forehead slowly faded and by the time Ma and Tanya returned with the tea he was sitting on Abbi's knee next to Nan and was beginning to talk to her.

But there was a whole barrage of questions burning on Abbi's lips.

'Why are you here, Nan? How did Tanya find you? What's going to happen to us? How's Mum? When are we going to see her again? When is she coming out of hospital?'

But no one answered her questions. Instead, Tanya smiled.

'Drink up,' she said, 'and we'll go and see her now.'

As soon as they left Ma Peters' house, Abbi realised they were not going in the right direction for the hospital.

'Hey, what's going on?' she demanded.

Tanya smiled at her in her rearview mirror.

'Don't worry,' she said. 'All will be revealed very shortly.'

Was Mum out of hospital? Was that it? But where was she?

Jordan was edgy again.

'I want to see my mum,' he grumbled.

Abbi put her arm round him, but he shrugged her off this time. She gazed intently out of the window and tried to recognise the streets, but even when they slowed down in front of a newly built block of flats, she had no idea where they were. It was coming over her again, this feeling she got, not being able to trust anyone. Not even her nan?

They climbed out of Tanya's car.

'I'll come back in a couple of hours,' said Tanya, behind the wheel.

'OK,' said Nan.

Then they were all hurrying through a light rain that had begun to fall, into the flats.

'Where...?' Abbi began.

'I live here now,' said Nan.

'But I didn't realise,' said Abbi. 'How come I managed to ring you?'

'I took my old phone number with me, when I moved,' said Nan.

Disappointment hit Abbi hard. One day, she had hoped to go back to the old house where she had spent so many happy hours as a child.

'Oh,' she said as the lift, spotlessly clean and sparkling, took them to the fourth floor.

There was an open hallway with three doors off. Nan took out her key and opened the green one.

'Welcome to my new home,' said Nan and they all walked in.

But it was like an Aladdin's cave inside. There were Nan's old furniture and cushions and ornaments all waiting to be re-explored. Abbi's disappointment disappeared instantly. She rushed around, excitedly picking up things she remembered from way back. She felt like a little girl again.

'Look,' she cried, dragging Jordan along with her. 'This china lady – I dropped her, didn't I? Yes, here's the crack where Nan stuck her together. And here's this dog – I used to make him a kennel out of cardboard boxes. And, I don't believe it – I used to play for hours with this squashy old frog, and—'

She froze. She sensed someone else had come into the room. She whipped round.

'Mum!'

Chapter Thirteen

Mum looked very pale and thin. Abbi experienced a rush of happiness as she stepped forward to kiss her. Mum hugged her, but Abbi felt no strength in Mum's arms.

'I'm going into a clinic,' Mum announced in a shaky voice.

'When?' asked Abbi, her heart thumping anxiously.

'In an hour or two.'

Abbi's roller-coaster of emotions hit bottom again. She had missed Mum more than she could say. Now she was going to lose her again, although she had to admit to herself that she knew it was the only way.

'What's a clinic?' asked Jordan.

'It's like a kind of hospital,' said Mum. 'It's going to make me better.'

'Can we come?'

Mum laughed, but Abbi didn't hear much humour in her voice.

'No, Jordan, I wish you could,' said Mum, shaking her head.

Jordan began to cry and threw himself at Mum, who looked like she was about to collapse.

'Please!' he cried.

Mum looked at Abbi over the top of Jordan's head.

'I have to do it on my own. I promised myself and the doctor at the hospital. That was the only reason they let me out of there so soon. And I promised your nan.' She smiled at her mother. 'This is sort of what we rowed about all those years ago. She was right, of course. I know that now. And we've all got to make up for the lost years.'

Abbi gently pulled Jordan away and sat him on her knee. She was going to hate being separated from Mum, but she had to admit it was what she had wanted her to do for ages. And there was another bonus about this. Mum and Nan seemed to have made up! So it wasn't all bad.

'How long is it for?' Abbi asked.

'A few weeks...'

'A few weeks?' Abbi gasped. She had imagined a few days would be enough.

'But won't we see you at all in that time?'

'Not much,' said Mum, tears springing in her eyes. 'But it's for the best.'

'Yeah,' Abbi said. 'We'll look after each other while we wait for you, won't we, Jordan?'

'I suppose so.'

'So what happens to us?' Abbi asked.

'You're coming here to live with me,' said Nan.

Abbi smiled and felt a shudder of relief pass up her spine.

'Great!' she said.

Ma was very nice, but coming to live with Nan was a much, much better idea.

Abbi sat close to Mum for a while.

'I've made so many promises to you, haven't I?' said Mum. 'I bet you don't believe I'm going to go through with it, do you?'

Abbi didn't reply. She wanted Mum to succeed, more than anything else in the world, but how could she be certain she would?

'This time,' said Mum, 'it will be a complete break. That's why I have to go right away. But my cure will only be complete if I can keep off all alcohol forever afterwards. That's my aim.'

An hour later, Tanya returned and Abbi found herself saying goodbye to Mum. She felt torn in half. One part desperately wanted Mum to stay, but the other part knew it was their only chance.

Surprisingly, the weeks passed quite quickly living with Nan, and Abbi counted the days until Mum would return. She was coping better with school now, partly because Miss Cook had left her alone and Will seemed to be as keen as ever to support her, although she was always wary of Charlie, Ellie and Grace, who were still ready to take advantage of her whenever they could.

In PSHE with Mr Lam, they had been discussing various issues that affect people's lives. So one day, Abbi made a decision. The following week, she stood facing the class, feeling extremely nervous, but determined. She looked at all those expectant faces and her legs almost gave way. How were they going to react to what she was about to say?

'You're sure you want to do this?' Mr Lam whispered from his seat beside her.

She nodded. She had thought long and hard about it, but she had always come to the same conclusion. She wanted to come clean.

'Right.' Mr Lam spoke to the rest of the class. 'This lesson is given over to Abbi Arnold, who has asked to talk to you all.'

Abbi saw Charlie and Ellie nudge each other and snigger, then Grace giggled. Several others looked at each other with raised eyebrows, but she had to go through with it. What was she hoping to achieve? Partly, it was her need to clarify everything in her own mind, to explain it all to Will, but it was also to do with those girls who had helped to make her life hell. She wanted them to understand.

'OK,' she began, wringing her hands together in front of her and trembling all over. She could hear the quake in her voice and she coughed to clear her throat. 'My mum has been an alcoholic for a number of years.'

Grace gasped loudly and the smirks were wiped in an instant from the faces of Charlie and Ellie.

'I want you all to imagine you're me,' said Abbi, not looking at anyone in particular.

For the next fifteen minutes, she held their attention. She told them everything. It seemed that the more she admitted, got it off her chest, as her nan would say, the better she felt.

When she had finished, she heard the silence in the room. Then suddenly, someone clapped, making Abbi jump. Then someone else started. Were they taking the mickey? But Mr Lam began clapping, too, and more and more of the class, until all except Charlie, Ellie and Grace had joined in. Abbi leant on the desk at the front of the class, amazed.

'Well,' said Mr Lam when the noise died down.

'I think we'll all agree that took an enormous amount of courage from Abbi to tell us her tale.'

Luckily, it was last period of the day and Abbi was able to escape, but before she reached the gate, Will caught up with her.

'Wow!' he said. 'You nearly had me crying back there!'

Abbi glanced at him, to make sure he wasn't joking. But he was dead serious. She was puzzled at him, yet again. She frowned.

'Why?' she asked.

'I never told you how I knew, did I?'

'No!' said Abbi. 'You didn't. You always managed to escape as I was about to ask you, but I've always wondered. So?'

'So,' said Will with a big grin. 'I'll tell you. Do you fancy a coke? In that burger bar on the corner?'

Abbi's heart somersaulted. Was he asking her for a date? Will, the handsome hunk that everyone, even sad old maths teachers, fell for? She felt her face glowing.

'Why not?'

Ten minutes later they were sitting opposite each other, coke bottles in their hands, neither of them willing to open the conversation.

'Well?' said Abbi at last.

She took a swig, but didn't take her eyes off Will's face, waiting for him to explain himself.

'Your mum and my mum,' he said. 'Exactly the same. I knew just what you were going through because I've been through it myself.'

Abbi gasped.

'You mean ... booze?'

Will nodded.

'Wow! Is she OK now?'

He nodded again.

'Brilliant!' he said. 'It's four years since she went into the clinic to dry out – and what I wanted to say was, it worked, Abbi. We've had our ups and downs since then, but I'm sure it's going to be OK for you, too.'

He had reached forward and was touching her hand. Abbi felt weak at the knees, but she managed a smile. He was smiling back at her, his eyes bright in his handsome face.

'I hope so, Will,' she said.

Life was definitely going to be so much better, thanks to Will and Nan.

But best of all, it looked as if her wishes were about to come true. Jordan and she would be keeping Mum, for good.

If you enjoyed reading *Keeping Mum*, look out for this title in the *Go For It!* series.

● ● ● ● ● ● ● ● ● ● ● ● ● ● ● ●

Moving On by Sue Vyner

Martin sat up. His body tense.

'What is it?' he said. Seriously worried now.

'It's – Grandad,' Dad said.

'Grandad?' Martin said.

'He's – gone Martin,' Dad said. Gulping.

'Gone? *Gone?*' Martin said. Thinking, *Where?* Where had Grandad gone on a Sunday morning? Some small part of him already registering something he didn't want to think.

'He's – Grandad's – died, Martin,' Dad said, and grabbed hold of Martin's hand.

Martin stared down at Dad's hand gripping his. Thinking. Well that was pretty clear. No way round that. Followed by, *no*. It couldn't be true. He'd seen Grandad on Friday. Two days ago. And he was fine. Grandad couldn't have – *died*. He couldn't even get his head round that word.

But then, seeing the bereft look on Dad's face, he thought it must be true.

He felt – dazed.

Nobody could be here one day and gone the next – could they?

For what seemed like a long while his brain didn't function. And then, when it did, thoughts came crashing through his head in a jumbled panic. He didn't know what to think or what to do or what to say. What *could* he say to something like this? How on earth was he expected to react?

All he knew was that a pain had grabbed his insides. Sitting there on the bed, with Dad still gripping his hand, he felt a pain he'd never experienced before. As if something had got a hold on him inside and was squeezing the breath out of him.

Dad suddenly let go of his hand and stood up. Moving nervously from one foot to the other.

'I've got to go back now, Martin. Things to do. But Mum'll come home now. Are you going to be all right?'

Martin nodded.

When Dad had gone, he got out of bed. Got dressed, like any other day. But feeling that it was wrong to be doing anything so normal.

When Mum came home, he was downstairs, slouched in a chair. She came up and kneeled on the floor in front of him. Gripped his hands. But he pulled them away, and folded his arms. Refusing to even look at her. She was going to tell him the same thing, wasn't she? And he didn't want to hear it again.

Mum started talking anyway. Telling him how they'd rung Grandad. And when there was no reply, how they'd gone down to the bungalow. And found him.

'He was – dead – love,' she said. Saying the word the same way Dad had, and the way he'd *thought* it. A word that was really difficult to get out of your mouth, or get your head round.

For a while, then, she stopped talking and all he could hear was her breathing.

Then she started again. Telling him, as though she had to convince him, how Grandad had died in his sleep, in his bed. And how when they'd found him he looked just like he was still sleeping.

'He looked so peaceful, love,' he heard her say.

But he couldn't bear it! He got up and started pacing round the room. Getting more and more agitated.

'I saw him on Friday and he was fine!' he protested, then caught his breath. Remembering how he'd told Grandad he'd go and play chess with him yesterday and how he'd gone to Andy's instead. He stopped pacing, and stood stock still. He clasped his head in his hands.

'If I'd gone yesterday, like I said I would,' he said wildly, 'I would've seen something was wrong with him.

He could've gone to hospital. He would've been all right. I didn't even ring him and tell him I wasn't going.'

He flopped back on the chair and dropped his head into his hands.

'But you couldn't have done anything, love,' Mum said fiercely, putting her arms round him. '*I* talked to him yesterday and he was fine. I told him where you'd gone. And he was fine about that too.' She stroked his back. Up and down. Up and down. Then she started talking again. More gently now. 'It must have been very sudden, love. A devastating stroke, or a massive heart attack. The doctor said it would've been *like the lights going out.* Grandad wouldn't have suffered.'